THE BILLIONAIRE & THE BARFLY

A New Adult Romance by
Adrianne James

Coming Home

THE BILLIONAIRE & THE BARFLY

A Coming Home Novel

by
Adrianne James
Copyright 2014 by Adrianne James
Published by Star Bound Books

Find Adrianne James on the web!
http://www.AdrianneJames.com
http://twitter.com/Adrianne_james
http://www.facebook.com/AuthorAdrianneJames
http://www.goodreads.com/AdrianneJames
Cover Design by Gonet Design
http://www.facebook.com/gonetdesign
Editing by Rogena Mitchell-Jones Manuscript Services
http://www.RogenaMitchell.com

Acknowledgements

Writing a book is one thing. Getting it ready for publication is completely different. There may be some authors out there who can go it completely alone, but I am not one of them. Because of that, I have a whole big list of 'thank you's to get through.

Thank you to my beta readers. You all know who you are and I adore each and every one of you for sticking with me and helping me with this little love story.

Thank you to Rogena, my brilliant editor who indulges me when I stress over a single typo in a sixty thousand word novel.

Thank you to Rachel, my publicist who got this gem into the hands of bloggers and reviewers.

Thank you to all the bloggers and reviewers who helped me spread the word.

Thank you to my husband, for everything you do including keeping the children occupied so I can write naughty scenes.

And a final thank you to my bestie, who always gives me the kick in the rear I need, when I need it.

Chapter One

The music was pumping through the large dark room filled with people. Lights were flashing and circling around, illuminating the dance floor in a kaleidoscope of colors. Aubrey Vincent laughed as she swayed to the music with some guy who came up behind her. She never minded when men joined her on the dance floor. It was more fun to dance with a partner anyway, and since she always showed up to bars alone, she welcomed the attention.

She had been in New York City for almost a week, and it had been constant work from the time her alarm went off before the sun until she went to bed. Being a personal assistant had its perks, traveling all across the world, for example, but it was also more than a full time job. Jenna worked round the clock for Viola Gaming Industries trying to acquire new clients and the next 'it' game. So when Jenna told Aubrey to go out and enjoy the city, she wasn't going to argue.

The bar was right in Times Square, and it was just as amazing as she had imagined it would be. People were everywhere, and the buildings lit up the area so bright it was almost like day time. In the three years that Aubrey had worked for Jenna, they had been to a number of places, but never New York City. For hours that afternoon, she had wandered the streets. She made sure to fully experience everything a tourist was supposed to do. After taking all of her shopping bags back to her hotel room, she ended the night in Times Square, and at the bar on every search engine listed as the place to be at night.

Aubrey turned to look at the man dancing behind her. She continued to sway her hips from side to side and trace her arms along her body to the beat of the music, but she was no longer interested in continuing to dance with the guy. She made no attempts to hide her shallow side. Looks weren't everything when it came to relationships, but when all she was looking for was a fun and fulfilling night out in a city she wouldn't step foot in again for who knows how long, looks mattered. Aubrey leaned in and spoke into his ear so he could hear her. "Thanks for the dance."

She smiled at him and walked away with a little wave. She could see the slight disappointment in his eyes, for all of the two seconds it took it to land on another girl wearing a tiny skirt and shaking her ass just in front of him. Aubrey gave a little laugh and made her way through the throng of people to the bar.

She ordered a Jack and cherry coke and turned to watch the world around her. When the bartender handed her the glass, he told her that the gentleman at the end of the bar had covered her tab. Smiling, Aubrey looked in the direction the bartender had pointed to see a tall blonde guy surrounded by women. His hair was gelled up in a messy guy-do, and he had on a superman t-shirt under a blazer. She wasn't sure if he were trying to be ironic or not, but he had on dark rimmed glasses, as well. When the man looked up at her, he smiled a brilliant smile and nodded his head as he lifted his own glass. She smiled and nodded back in thanks, but she wouldn't go over to him.

He may have that hot geek thing going on, but she wasn't one to fight for a guy's attention, and by the way those girls were already eyeing her, she would have had to. No thank you. Taking her drink, she made her way back to the dance floor and spotted him—the perfect memory for New York City—tall, with jet black hair, and a body to die for. Aubrey walked straight to him. She wasn't shy, she wasn't subtle, and she knew what she wanted. When she stood in front of him, Aubrey took a big gulp of her drink and sat it on the table where he stood, and then took his hand, leading him to the dance floor. She didn't ask, and he didn't protest.

Aubrey and the tall hottie danced and drank together until the bar closed. Walking out the door into the night, she was once again surprised that it didn't look much like night. She grasped his hand in hers.

"You live around here?" she asked with a flirty smile. When his eyes lit up, she knew she had him.

"No, but my hotel is just a few blocks away, unless you would rather go to yours?"

"Nope, yours is just fine."

Tall Hottie, as Aubrey began referring to him as in her head, was staying in some high rise hotel just a few blocks from Time Square. The elevator even had a bell man. He was rather professional, not even looking when Tall Hottie began kissing and fondling her before they even reached his floor.

Aubrey and her man of the night stumbled from the elevator, completely entwined with one another—hands, legs, lips. Her back pressed up against a door with a thud as Tall Hottie wrestled with his keys and tried to unlock the door without removing his mouth from her skin.

The door fell open, sending them both tumbling into the room laughing. It could have been seen as an utter disaster, falling on the floor and bumping their heads, but Aubrey didn't care. She loved when things didn't go picture perfect. Nothing was, and if they could laugh it off, then why ruin the night?

"I am so sorry," he said.

"Don't be," she replied, then leaned up and kissed him. Aubrey heard the door close behind her and Tall Hottie moved, straddling her with a knee on either side of her hips before he pulled away from her kiss.

"Do you have a condom?" She was shocked at his question. Of course, she did, but why didn't he? She never fucked without protection. She wasn't stupid. Maybe he hadn't intended on bringing a girl back to his room, but what if she didn't? Would he stop then or keep going and hope for the best?

"Of course I do. In my purse." Tall Hottie moved off her and stood, then reached down to grab her hand and help her up off the floor. Once they were standing, he leaned in and kissed her softly before walking over to the little fridge in the corner of the room.

"Want a drink?" he asked. She was digging into the little secret zip pocket in her purse for her condom stash. She pulled two out hoping he might be one of those guys who could go twice in a row. Wouldn't that be her lucky night? She had only met one man who could do that before, but unfortunately, even with him getting off twice, he couldn't get her off once. It was such a waste.

"Just water. I had plenty at the bar." Aubrey held up the shiny silver foil packets in her hand and dropped her purse to the ground. She was under no delusion that they were going to hang out, chit chat, and get to know each other. She walked over to him and took the bottle of water from his hand before taking a sip.

Tall Hottie watched her as she strolled across the room to the perfectly made bed. Aubrey sat on the edge and began to take her shoes off. Once Tall Hottie saw her beginning to undress, he turned into Speedy Gonzolas and was naked before she even managed to get her zipper down.

He was a glorious specimen. More abs than she could count, and the perfect V leading directly to his dark curls that framed his very big and very hard dick. He strode over to her with confidence. She hoped he was as confident in bed as he was in his appearance.

Aubrey let him undress her, caress her, and lay her back on the bed. When her body started to react to his, she shut her mind off and just enjoyed the feeling of sexual euphoria.

~*~

Tall Hottie stood and walked to the bathroom to clean up, or so she assumed. She didn't ask. She honestly didn't care. He got her off, and that's all she came for. Aubrey walked around the room and picked up her clothing, putting each piece on as she found it. By the time Tall Hottie walked back out of the bathroom, still in all his naked glory, she was completely dressed.

"Going so soon? You can stay if you want. I mean, this hotel has a kick ass breakfast buffet," then he looked at the clock over his shoulder showing three twenty-two, "I mean, it will start serving in a little over two hours."

"Sorry, but I have to go. This was fun." Aubrey walked to the door and opened it. Tall Hottie slipped his boxers on and walked over to her.

"It was. When are you leaving New York?" She could see the hopeful look in his eye. He was an okay lover, he got the job done after all, but she didn't even know his name and didn't want to. She had learned to accept this about herself long ago. She wasn't the type who equated sex with love. Sex was sex, a physical need and a pleasurable release. Love and sex could and did go hand in hand, but it didn't have to. Making love and having sex were completely different.

"Soon. Have a good trip," Aubrey said then walked out and closed the door behind her. She pressed the elevator button down the hall and adjusted the straps on her dress. She fingered her hair to tame the bed head look down a notch just as the elevator door opened.

Aubrey came face to face with the same blonde who bought her drink earlier. Only he was alone. He must have had his fun in one of the ladies' rooms. Good for him. She smiled and nodded at him and stepped in. She turned to face the doors and rode the elevator down in silence. Should she thank him for the drink? Did he even realize that she was that girl or were there so many that he lost track? Not that it mattered. She only had a few floors left to go.

The doors opened, and she quickly took her leave. Awkward silences weren't her thing. She thought for a second she heard him say something, but when she turned back to ask what it was, the elevator had closed, and he was gone.

The lobby was empty except for a security guard behind a desk. She didn't know where she was or how to get back to her hotel. She may not be from the city, but she knew enough to know that wandering around at three in the morning wasn't such a good idea.

"Excuse me?" she asked as she approached the desk. The security guard stood up quickly and looked around before looking at her.

"Yes, can I help you?" he asked.

"Do you mind telling me what the address of this hotel is so I can call a taxi?"

"You don't know where you are? Are you okay?"

"I'm fine. I just need the address, or even the name of the hotel." Aubrey knew that he was just doing his job, but she was fine, and getting really tired. She just wanted to go to bed in her own hotel room.

"Let me call a cab for you. We have a company on file we use for our guests. They can take you wherever you need to go."

"Thank you." She was going to protest. She could call her own cab if she knew where she was, but figured it was easier to just let the man call. She could give into the macho thing once in a while if it actually made things easier.

The security guard picked up the phone and began punching in numbers. Aubrey took the opportunity to walk around the waiting room. There were fancy pieces of artwork all over the walls and lots of glass decor and leather seating. Swanky was the word that came to mind when Aubrey tried to think of a word to describe it. *The Tall Hottie in the Swanky Hotel.* She laughed to herself a little. She loved that she could find little things like that to laugh about. She never wanted to go a day without laughing. Her grandmother used to always say that laughter was the best medicine. She believed that fully. She tried to find something to laugh at every day. Some days were harder than others, but even if she had the worst day in the history of days, a small laugh would help relieve the stress just a little.

"Car's here." Aubrey turned and smiled at the guard, and with a little wave goodbye, she headed out to the waiting cab. Aubrey gave the driver the name of her hotel and leaned back in her seat, closing her eyes. It had been a long night, and her morning was going to come all too soon.

Chapter Two

Morning came much too early for Aubrey, but if she were anything, she was professional. Three hours of sleep, a hot shower, a cup of coffee, and she was ready to go. Not that she had to go far. When she and Jenna traveled trying to gain new business, they worked from either Jenna's hotel room or a conference room that the hotel would provide for them when they had meetings. That morning, they were in the conference room. They were supposed to have a meeting.

Unfortunately for them, Donavon Sports, a new start up company, was a no-show. They were the next *it* company in sports apparel, and Viola Gaming Industries wanted to use their logo on the characters in a new game. They wanted to cross market. They wanted a lot that they were willing to pay for. Too bad the company didn't see it the same way.

Jenna was talking fast and furiously with her contact at Donavon to find out what had happened. Aubrey could only hear one side of the conversation, but it wasn't good. They were too late. Maximus Gaming strikes again.

"Damn it, Josie. We could have beaten whatever offer Maximus gave you. You should have called us, given us a chance. We have been in this industry for thirty years. Maximus is practically brand new. They don't have the experience we do

"I know they developed the newest gaming system but—" Jenna continued on with her pitch that had become perfected over the last few months. Aubrey found the papers with market data that stated users of old gaming systems still purchased games and more often than those who were upgrading to new systems. It was a numbers game, and in today's market, money, and lack of money, was everything.

Aubrey quickly handed Jenna the papers with the data, and also another on the legal aspects of breaking a verbal contract (hoping that Maximus might have forgotten to bring the paper with the dotted line) before slipping out the door. Jenna was going to need a fresh coffee after that phone call, and she wanted to make sure to have it ready for her. Aubrey used her cell on the way to the coffee shop to call and make the travel arrangements for their flight home that night. On the way back, she called the top three other sports apparel companies in the city and set up impromptu meetings for Jenna. The best way to impress the boss was to always be a step or two ahead of the game.

If she ever wanted to get out of her parents attic and able to move to a city, being a step ahead was a good thing. She loved working for Jenna, but she had bigger aspirations than being a personal assistant. She

knew others whose career path was being a personal
assistant, but that wasn't hers. No, she wanted her own
PA someday.

Jenna was off the phone when Aubrey walked in.
She handed her the coffee and waited for a minute
before informing her of the rest of the day's plans.

"Thank you, I needed that. Maximus screwed us
again. We need to make some calls. If we go back and
don't have a contract in hand, my ass is going to be
eaten alive."

"We have three appointments—Vincent at eleven,
Berkins at one, and Leslie at three. Our flight home is
at six forty five. You have time to finish your coffee,
and I will organize these papers and have everything
ready to go by ten. A cab will be outside and waiting
for us."

"I swear I would be lost without you, Aubrey."
Jenna said. When she walked out of the conference
room, Aubrey let out a sigh. It was great to be needed
and good at a job, but she was waiting for the day that
she was given more. Anything more. What did she
have to do to prove that to Viola Gaming? She had
been with the company for five years. Two as the mail
room copy girl and the last three as Jenna's personal
assistant. It was quite a jump from sorting envelopes to
traveling the world with the head of new acquisitions,
but once she got a taste of what Jenna did daily, she
knew she needed to be in that line of work. She would
be good at it. She knew how to talk to people and how
to get them to see her way. That's all it was really—
being a good sales person.

"Yes, Jenna, you would," she muttered to herself as she cleaned up the papers strewn all over the table.

~*~

The first two meetings went just about as well as the no show. Apparently, Maximus had an exclusivity clause in their contract. Even though they were making football games, and Viola was looking to make a line of sports games for girls that included softball, volleyball, and field hockey, they couldn't sign on.

Needless to say, Aubrey was rather irritated as she searched online on her phone as the cab driver took them to their third and final meeting of the day. If Leslie were already signed with Maximus, she would have to start calling smaller companies and make phone appointments or push back their flight.

Jenna sat beside her absolutely silent. She got that way when she was worried. Usually, Aubrey would tell her it would be okay and remind her of how much other business they had acquired on their trip. Only this time, they hadn't gotten anything. The last two trips were the same.

The cab pulled up in front of a tall building with Leslie's Athletics in big bold letters across the front. Aubrey paid the cab driver, and the two women stepped out and crossed their fingers that Maximus wasn't inside wooing them with their fancy new systems and iron clad contracts.

Aubrey and Jenna were met at the door by a very fit woman. She had to have been more toned than any other woman Aubrey had met before. She wasn't a body builder by any means, but each and every one of her visible muscles were defined.

"Welcome!" the woman beamed at them, "Thank you so much for coming to see us today. I'm Leslie Hunter."

Aubrey was taken aback. She had never met with an owner of a company before. Usually, they sent people like her and Jenna to meet with them, people who were hired, so the owner didn't have to worry about little stuff. Well, little in the scope of the entire business.

"It is so nice to meet you, Leslie. My name is Jenna Peterson, and this is my assistant Aubrey Vincent. Thank you for seeing us on such short notice."

The three women walked into the large building that definitely held a woman's touch. It wasn't girly, but it was well decorated, and the artwork with big muscular men was kept to a minimum. Most sports companies Aubrey had visited had been really into athletic art. This building had images of people winning races, before and after pictures of employees, and a ton of children.

"I love the decor in here. Are these children of employees?" Aubrey asked, trying to make conversation besides the sale. Make a connection to your consumer and making the sale is so much easier. Sales 101.

"Actually these are all children with disabilities who have found sports and activities to help them in their treatments or just to give them something to do to feel normal. We have a foundation that connects personal coaches with these kids. They each receive a gift card for new equipment and apparel and a year of coaching. These are our kids."

Aubrey was blown away. She had never met a more generous company before. It warmed her heart to know that at least someone actually existed that cared for complete strangers. She hadn't found any in a long time.

"That must be a very costly charity, but I have never heard about it. Where do you advertise it?" Jenna asked. She didn't get it. It wasn't about the money or the prestige of the charity.

"Because we don't advertise it. It isn't about growing Leslie's Apparel, but about helping these kids."

"But how do you fund it?" Jenna asked, still completely confused. Aubrey knew she needed to jump in and get Jenna to stop talking if they planned on getting the sale at all. Sales 101 rule number two: don't insult the consumer.

"Jenna, what she is saying is that they fund it from their profits. But they don't advertise it because they don't want to exploit what they are doing. They don't do it for the acclaim, but because it's a good thing to do. They earn a little less, but it's worth it to them."

"That is exactly right, Aubrey. Now, shall we head into the conference room? I am really interested in this all woman's sports line of games. That's something new, and I am all about empowering women and encouraging girls to become more active. You know a game where the girls are dressed."

Aubrey gave a little laugh even though it wasn't funny. It was one of the reasons that Viola was launching a new line. A panel of women employees, as well as a street survey, both revealed that many women would be more interested in video games if the women characters were more than eye candy for the male players. Even the games where the women were warriors, they were barely dressed while the male characters were clad in leather and armor.

"Absolutely. And if you are interested, the characters will all be wearing Leslie's Apparel," Jenna said. She was back in the game, and Aubrey knew this was where she stepped back and just took notes.

An hour later, Aubrey walked out of the building behind Jenna and Leslie. The excitement was bubbling inside of her, and she couldn't wait until they were safely in the cab to let it out in a very unprofessional scream of joy.

"Thank you again. The final contracts will be signed and sent to your office in the morning," Leslie said, and then shook Jenna's hand. Jenna responded with a thank you of her own and opened the cab door.

Aubrey smiled at Leslie and moved to get in the cab when Leslie placed a hand on her arm. Stopping, she turned to look at her.

"Thank you, too. You keep working hard, and this one will eventually have to move you up, even if she won't be able to find another assistant quite like you."

"Thank you. You and this company are an inspiration. I hope to have your success one day."

"I'm sorry, but we have to head out now. Our flight leaves in just a few hours. Aubrey," Jenna said then nodded toward the cab. Aubrey shook Leslie's hand, even when she really wanted to hug her, and climbed into the cab. A few more words were shared between the women outside, and then Jenna climbed in after her.

As soon as the cab had pulled away from the curb, both women cheered. They had done it. Not only had they secured an apparel line, but also it seemed it was the perfect one after all. Maybe they should thank Maximus for their ninja like skills just this once. If they had signed with any of the other companies, they would have lost out on what seemed like the perfect match.

Chapter Three

Aubrey woke up covered in sweat. It was always incredibly and horribly hot in her bedroom. Unless it was winter, then it was practically an ice cube. She had two fans already on but flipped the switch on a third. She looked out the window to see that the sky was barely tinted pink and wondered why on earth she was awake. The heat didn't wake her. She had grown used to that over the years. After all, her bedroom was in her parent's attic and had been since she was sixteen.

When she heard the yelling coming through the floors, she knew why she was awake. Her younger brother was fighting with her parents again. What she didn't know was why it was happening at the butt crack of dawn. She would be so glad when she could move out and into her own apartment in the city. She was close. She had been saving since she became Jenna's assistant. But living in the city was more expensive than she had ever realized.

She had already moved out twice before. Both times she made a big deal out of leaving and being grown and ready and not needing her parents help. Both times had been utter failures sending her back to the damn attic with her tail between her legs. But that was who she used to be. She failed at everything she did, except high school—she was definitely not a failure in High School, until Viola. With Viola, she had learned her strengths and learned to play them up. She knew that things would be different when she moved out next time. They had to be. She couldn't take it if they weren't.

Aubrey dove back into her bed and stuffed her head under her pillows hoping to block out the noise coming from downstairs. For a brief moment, she thought it worked. And technically, it had. The noise was no longer coming from downstairs. Her brother had decided to come and bang on her door.

Aubrey threw the pillow at the door, not that it would actually do anything, but it felt good to throw something. She was tired. The plane hadn't landed until almost midnight after some stupid delay, and then it took another hour and a half to get home. Aubrey sat up and padded to the door, and swung it open to see that she was right. Ben stood there, looking completely exasperated.

Most of the time, she was glad for the close relationship they had. They weren't close in age, but it had never mattered. She was there when he needed her, and he was there for her. Aubrey stepped back and let him come in, then closed the door behind him.

"What happened this time?" she asked through a yawn. Aubrey climbed back into her bed and sat, waiting for him to go into the typical tirade. Most of the time, she could understand both sides of the argument. She tried to be the peace keeper between her less than perfect brother and her slightly over protective parents. Sometimes it worked, sometimes it didn't.

"They are completely over reacting. I broke curfew, it's not like I stole the car." That was when Aubrey really looked at her brother, not through sleep filled eyes, but actually looked. He was completely dressed. She looked back out the window and squinted at her clock. He had been out all night. It was five in the morning, and he just got home. It was no wonder that their parents flipped their lids.

"Ben, you have got to be kidding me! You just got home, and you think they are overreacting? Sorry, this one I can not argue for you. Where were you?"

"I thought you would understand. You used to stay out all night, too. Do you even remember or are you too old to actually get it anymore? You know what, forget it." Ben stood and left her room, and slammed her door behind him. With a huff, she fell back to lie in bed. She would deal with that mess later. Or she would just let him be mad and ignore her for a few days. At least then she could get some damn sleep.

After struggling to fall back asleep for over an hour, she gave up. Jenna had told her to take the morning off and rest up, but she figured she might as well head in. She wanted everyone to see her dedication to her job and to the company.

After a quick shower and a banana on the way out the door, Aubrey started the hour long drive into the city. She had two weeks before the next trip, and Aubrey had a ton of organizing to do in the mean time.

The music flowed through her car as she mentally started working on her to-do list. Meetings had to be set, flights scheduled, hotels booked. Not to mention dinner reservations made for current clients and Jenna's over all errands that were never ending. She needed to find new sources for market research and make a ton of copies.

It was going to be one long day.

The office was buzzing with activity when she walked in. She wasn't sure what was going on, but from the worried looks on everyone's faces, it wasn't a good thing. Rushing to her desk, she managed to overhear the name Maximus and her heart fell. Could they have swooped in and managed to undo the work that she and Jenna had done with Leslie already?

Aubrey placed her purse on her desk and peered through Jenna's glass office wall. She was on the phone and pacing the room, her arms swinging wildly, and her face turning redder and redder as the seconds ticked by. Aubrey quickly got a bottle of water from the refrigerator around the corner and a hot cup of coffee as well as two aspirin and headed back to Jenna.

Aubrey knocked softly, knowing that she was still on the phone and opened the door slowly. Jenna gave her a quick nod of acknowledgement before turning her back to continue her tirade.

"Damn it, Mike. NO. We signed Leslie........ I know they are small, but...... Would you listen? Maximus cornered all the other companies in New York City. Would you rather we had come back empty handed? Plus, Leslie is a female brand. Sure they have a men's line, but they are female owned and operated. Plus, they have this charity that will help sell just about anything sports related."

Aubrey was annoyed that she brought up the charity. They had been told by Leslie herself that it wasn't for marketing purposes, but it wasn't her place to correct her boss. Jenna turned and faced Aubrey. She wasn't sure if she should leave or stay. Would she be needed or not? She tried to give her a questioning look, but Jenna had walked away and opened the door. There was her answer.

Aubrey high tailed it out of the room, but not before hearing Jenna say the one thing she never thought she would. "Mike, Leslie was my idea. I know we saw them last, but that was Aubrey's fault."

The door clicked closed, and her heart sank. She had been thrown under the bus with the second most important person in the whole damn company. Aubrey sank into her desk chair and stared at the door, still trying to make sense of everything. She had done her job. She had booked the appointments, and she had saved Jenna from losing the contract over the charity… which, from the sound of it, was about to be thrown out anyway. Leslie would never agree to use the charity the way that Jenna intended. Aubrey thought she knew that.

At least, it was obvious to her. Deciding that moping wasn't going to actually make her look any better, she cleared her desk and got to work. In two weeks time, they would be meeting with the head of the women's soccer league, the top college's athletics divisions, and the United States Olympics committee. She wanted to be able to say that she was part of the project from conception through development and sales. She wanted to be the one to book the meetings and make sure that the contracts were in the right hands at the right times. Too bad Jenna would get all the credit for it.

~*~

By the end of the day, the commotion had calmed, and people were coming by every few minutes to congratulate Jenna on landing the perfect deal. Jenna never even said thank you. Typically, Aubrey felt the appreciation from her. She never thought of her as selfish or attention seeking, but for some reason, things were changing.

"Hey," Bridgette, Mike's assistant, said as she came down the hall. Aubrey looked up for the computer to see that it was already seven.

"Hey, heading out?"

"Yeah, you should, too. Hell of a day today. Congrats on Leslie."

"You know, you are the first to say that to me. But hey, I'm just an assistant, right?"

"I know you, and I know Jenna. You had more to do with that contract than she did. Just don't tell her I said that. Come on. Let's grab a drink and a bite to eat."

Aubrey agreed wholeheartedly when her stomach rumbled loudly. When she got in the zone, she tended to forget to eat. "Sounds like a plan."

The bar wasn't far from the office. Bridgette and Aubrey had gone there many times after work for a drink. Sometimes they would stick around and dance a bit, other times they had their one drink and headed home. Bridgette was the closest thing to a friend that Aubrey had at the office. She knew other people, and was friendly with them, but no one had actually cared to go out after work. Aubrey thought at first it was because she was the only one in the same age decade as Bridgette, but the more they hung out, the more she saw her trying to build a friendship.

It was time she tried to build one, too. She needed a girl friend. She had a million friends in high school. She hadn't realized when she had lost them. But she had. The only one who still kept in touch was Fiona, who was off at college doing the good girl thing and getting some degree or another. She never failed at anything.

"Have you ever had the food here? We won't get mad cow or anything, right?" Aubrey asked as she warily looked at the menu. It had burgers and wings and nachos and just a few other things that were either frozen or in a can when they came into the kitchen.

"I have. Stay away from the nachos, but the burger is pretty good."

The girls ordered their food and some drinks but instead of waiting at the table, they headed to the dance floor. Aubrey let loose whenever she was dancing. She didn't care what she looked like, even though she could dance. All she cared about was feeling the music flowing through her, feeling the emotions the songs were meant to induce. Most of the time, in a bar, it's more about energy and sex. But every once in a while, they would play something that had real meaning behind it, and Aubrey was always able to feel the meaning.

"OH! Food's here!" Bridgette yelled over the music, pointing to their table. Aubrey nodded and wiped the sweat from her brow. The two walked over, dodging dancing bodies the whole way.

"I'm going to go wash up first. Be right back," Aubrey said. Bridgette nodded and dug into her fries with a sigh. With a laugh, she walked toward the bathroom. There was no way she was about to eat covered in sweat. The least she could do was wash her hands.

She passed by the bar and had to stop. She turned to see the same man, or what looked like the same man, sitting on a bar stool watching her. The same hot blonde man with the stupid superman shirt—only this time he had on a batman belt. It had to be him. How many hot blonde superhero geeks were actually out there?

Aubrey continued to the bathroom to wash up, but made sure to make a note of where he was, so when she returned she could keep an eye on him. It was strange that he was in the same bar as her twice in the same week in two completely different cities, a thousand miles apart.

Why was he there? Had he followed her? Or did he actually have some reason to be there? She washed quickly and stormed out. She was going to ask him. Forget waiting around for him to be a creep. She wanted to know right then. Otherwise, she wouldn't be able to enjoy her dinner or her night dancing with Bridgette.

Hot Geeky Man (oh, the names she came up with for the men she didn't actually know) was still sitting at the bar and with his eyes still on her. The minute she opened the bathroom door she found his eyes watching her. She thought they were blue, but as she grew closer, she saw they were more of a slate grey. They were deep and captivating. Why did Hot Geeky Man have to possibly be a Hot Psycho Stalker?

"You were in New York City," she accused. Aubrey crossed her arms and stood in front of him. She stared down at him, liking the fact that while he was sitting she had the height advantage for a position of power.

"Yup, so were you." His voice was deep. In fact, it was a *so deep that you wanted to melt right there into a puddle of goo* kind of voice.

"Why are you here? Did you follow me?" She was trying to keep her voice from quivering. She wasn't sure if it was quivering out of the slight fear she had run through her or at how badly she wanted to launch herself at him. She needed to walk away before he said something sexy in that voice of his.

"Nope, didn't follow you. I could ask you the same thing." He had a point. If he hadn't followed her, perhaps that was why he was staring, to make sure that she wasn't the psycho.

"Fine, have a nice night." Aubrey turned and walked away quickly. She got back to the table with Bridgette and felt like a complete fool.

"What was that?" Bridgett asked between fries.

"Oh, that? Just me making a complete ass out of myself."

Chapter Four

Bridgette was right. The burgers were good. So good that she scarfed it down faster than she would have thought possible. Leaning back in her chair, she couldn't help but feel the prickles on the back of her neck. Someone was watching her. She turned her head slightly, trying to see who it was without being obvious.

What should have been obvious was that it was Hot Geeky Man who was staring. She didn't know what his issue was, but she wasn't having anything to do with it. Besides, three girls rocking dresses so short that their asses were practically falling out of them had already found him and clung to his side. She wasn't going back over there. She wasn't into cat fights.

"Come on, let's go dance!" Aubrey said, forcing herself to stop thinking about the blonde with the penetrating stare behind her. Bridgette agreed and followed her to the dance floor.

Once again, the music flowed through her. Aubrey closed her eyes and just felt it. Her body swayed about as the song came to an end, and she opened her eyes. Bridgette was dancing with some guy, cute guy—but so not the point, and right in front of her stood Hot Geeky Man.

Aubrey placed her hands against his chest and pushed him. Or tried to, but he didn't move very far. "What is your issue?" she yelled over the music.

"You looked so relaxed dancing that I had to join you. The only time I feel as relaxed as you look is when I'm sitting at home reading." His answer was honest. She could tell that from the innocence on his face. "Do you want to show me how to feel like that in the middle of this insane room with the music pounding so loudly I can barely hear myself think?"

"If you don't like it, why do you come?"

"I like beer on tap. The only place to get that is a bar. The small hole-in-the-wall bars don't have a big selection, and typically, they smell a little funky. I would rather deal with this insanity, have a good draft, and get to talk to you."

"Did you just say funky?" she laughed.

"I did. Would you prefer gag-worthy? How about gross? Stinky? Icky? Nasty?" The smile on his face was enough to light the room, and make her agree to a dance.

"Okay, okay. Let's dance."

~*~

He was a horrible dancer. Aubrey tried to help him find the beat. She placed her hands on his hips and moved them side to side. The minute she let go, he lost it. She tried to turn so her back was to his front, wrapped his arms around her waist, and dancing for him. Having him just use her body as a guide. All that did was serve to turn her on (the man had to be hiding some killer abs under that t-shirt) and prove that even with a guide, he couldn't keep a beat to save his life.

"Okay, okay, I think I give up," he said, throwing his hands in the air.

"Don't give up. You can keep trying. You don't have to be a good dancer to enjoy dancing. Let's take a break and grab a drink." She led him off the floor, and then released his hand. She didn't want to. For the first time in the last hour, his hands weren't touching her in some way, and she felt their absence.

"Nate, two waters, please," Hot Geeky Man said to the bartender.

"You got it, Henry." Shit. Now she knew his name. She rather liked Hot Geeky Man. Knowing his name made it a little more real than a fun night. She hadn't intended to make it more than drinks and dancing, but somehow, knowing his name, made him more irresistible. *Shit.*

"So, since we never actually did the whole introduction thing and I can't keep calling you Diana Prince in my head—"

"Diana Prince? Where did that come from?" Did she look like an ex? Some girl he used to know? That was a nice little piece of info to keep reminding her of her own rule. No serious men in her life until she actually had more time to have a life. Like when she wasn't an assistant any longer, and when she had one of her own.

"Sorry, comic reference. Anyway, I'm Henry, and you are?"

"Aubrey."

"Well, Aubrey, it is very nice to meet you." Henry smiled that brilliant smile at her and handed her the glass of water. She smiled back and took it from him. By the time she took a sip and set her glass down on the bar top, two women had already appeared on the other side of Henry.

She was about to walk away, when he looked over his shoulder at her and mouthed 'help me'. She giggled a little and shook her head no. She wanted to see, and hear, what made this man such a magnet. Besides the killer smile, eyes, and hopefully perfect body. He hadn't talked to these girls, so they couldn't know how funny and charming he was—even if he were a grown man with a penchant for comic books.

Henry frowned at her and turned back to the girls. She listened as he tried to get away. He used everything from he had to pee to he needed to go. Finally, he played the ace card.

"Ladies, why don't I get the next couple rounds, because I hate to tell you this, but you just aren't my type, if you understand what I'm saying."

Aubrey had to hold back a laugh as she watched the looks on their faces fall. Then, a little petite red head leaned in and whispered something into his ear. He pulled back so fast the bar stool fell out from under him.

"No, that is quite all right. Enjoy the drinks. I am leaving now." Henry handed the bartender a stack of cash and turned to see a red faced Aubrey cackling away. The scowl that was on his face faded and was replaced with a grin. "Oh shush. You don't know what she said to me!"

"No, I don't. But I want to!"

"Fine, but don't say I didn't warn you."

Henry leaned in and whispered in her ear. The things he was saying were dirty for sure, but they had nothing on the way his breath felt tickling her ear or how his fingers softly tucked her hair behind her ear to begin with. She was only able to concentrate on the words he was saying when strap-on was mentioned.

She couldn't stop her laughter. What was this man's dick made out of? Gold?

"You have to tell me, what is it about you that has girls flocking to your side?"

"I'm not sure how to take that?"

"I mean, I know the obvious reasons, but this is something else entirely."

"I think I might just let you try and figure it out on your own. How about if we get out of here? Are you in the mood for a late night coffee?"

The night was beginning to border into date territory, but Aubrey couldn't help herself. The thought of walking away before she knew all she could about him was terrifying. What if she didn't see him again? She would stick to her rules—she would only spend one night with him. But she wanted to make it last.

"Let me just say bye to my friend real quick."

~*~

"You cannot be serious! You dunk donuts in milk or coffee. Not toast!" Henry said laughing. They had wound up at an all night coffee shop and were the only two in the place. Henry ordered his coffee with a ton of instructions, and Aubrey asked for black. She also ordered rye toast to go with it.

"Yes, toast. But only rye toast with tons of butter. My grandmother used to do it all the time. She finally let me try it when I was eight or so. It was the only time I was allowed coffee, and since everyone else in my family drank it, I wanted to, too. What's it called, oh! Acquiring a taste? Yes, Rye dipped in coffee is an acquired taste."

"Whatever you say," he said while still laughing at her peculiar tastes.

"Hey, I didn't say a word about your Froo-Froo coffee drink. Leave my toast alone."

Henry put his hands up in surrender. "Okay, Okay. No more teasing."

"Thank you."

"So, want to tell me why you came to the bar tonight?" he asked.

"Work bullshit, and I was hungry. Bridgette asked if I wanted to go, so I did."

"I would say I was sorry you had bullshit drama at work, but if it got you to the bar... and to me..."

Why did he have to keep saying things like that to her? Didn't he know that she wasn't one to fall for anyone? The flutter in her heart was violating her number one rule. No feelings. It was a choice she made. She knew she wanted more of him, but damn it, she didn't want to be thinking of him for days after, and if he continued to talk like that, she knew she would.

Aubrey leaned into him and placed her lips on his, very softly. Nothing that would be considered obscene, but it held a ton of promises. "Do you want to show me where you are staying tonight?"

She figured that if she cut all the mental bonding time, it would be easier. She hadn't planned on another one night stand so soon, but she was dying to see this man naked. It would get his words out of her head. It would. She was sure of it.

"Sorry, Aubrey, but no. I don't. Let me take you home." His words were full of defeat as if she had just failed some test she didn't know she was taking. She had never been shot down like that before. It stung.

"No, I can find my own way." She stood and left without another word.

She took a cab back to her office and climbed into her car. Once the engine turned over, she blared the music and drove off, taking her aggression out on the road.

Chapter Five

It had been a whole week. A whole damn week and Henry was still on her mind. Why did she go out for coffee with him? She knew better. Emotional connections were for people who didn't have to travel all the time, for people with time to actually have a relationship. For people who didn't suck at being a girlfriend. Aubrey was not one of those people.

Not that it mattered. He didn't want her after all.

In a single week, Aubrey went from high on life to Debbie downer. The job she loved to do and thought she was appreciated, no longer felt like that. She never felt like more of an assistant than she had that week. That one comment by Jenna ruined her whole perception of herself. She had thought she was needed and wanted. She was, but as a scape goat.

Then there was Henry. *Fucking Henry.* Why couldn't she get him out of her damn head? Why did she let him in to begin with?

Her car broke down, and she had to use a chunk of her savings to fix it. Her brother still wasn't speaking to her, and her mother decided it would be a grand idea to invite her ex-boyfriend (who she hated because he figured out sex was just sex way before she had and proceeded to put it into practice before telling her he no longer wanted to be exclusive) and his family over that weekend for a barbeque. Her mother really didn't get it.

Aubrey pressed the elevator button and watched the numbers light up as they descended each floor of the building. Viola was huge. There were twenty stories to the building and every office on every floor was in use. It was a company that valued its employees. Or at least that's what they boast. Viola may value her, but Jenna sure didn't.

The elevator doors opened, and Aubrey stepped in. It stopped on every floor on the way up to the sixteenth level. People piled in and out the whole way making a normal two minute trip take ten. Aubrey looked at her watch and groaned. She was late.

Rushing to her desk, she grabbed Jenna's coffee on the way, sloshing a little on her hand. "FUCK!" she yelled before dropping the mug to the tile floor where it shattered into a million pieces.

Everyone turned to look at her. She flushed red but let them know she was fine and sat her bag down on the table closest to her before cleaning up the mess.

With a fresh cup in hand, and a much slower gait, she walked into Jenna's office. The phone was pressed to her ear, and the look on her face told Aubrey it wasn't a good phone call. There were a few 'uh-huhs' and a couple 'yes sir's before she hung the phone up. Then the look was trained on Aubrey.

"You're late."

"I'm sorry, there was—"

"No, no excuses. Here is a list of everything I need done today. When you get back, I will have more." Jenna held out a slip of paper, effectively cutting the conversation off.

"Jenna, I really am sorry. Have I done something wrong?"

"Why would you ask that? Doing errands is part of your job. I just haven't utilized you in this way yet. I am paying you to assist me, and this is part of it. You are doing fine. Now, please get these done, and I will see you when you get back."

Aubrey took the slip from her and walked out the door. When she was seated at her desk, she opened the paper and wanted to cry. She had to walk Jenna's dog, drop off her dry cleaning, and pick up a box of tampons. Last week she had been Jenna's right hand. This week she was a damn dog walker.

It didn't matter. She would not fail at being a personal assistant after being so good at it for years. No, she would do as she was asked and not say another word about it. At least, not to Jenna.

~*~

Once Aubrey had left the building, she felt slightly better. When she drove to Jenna's house to get the dog, she wasn't so sure. Apparently Jenna's puppy wasn't exactly a puppy. No, the dog was a mastiff. A fucking dog almost as tall as she was.

Its crap piles were huge, too. Worst day of work ever.

Once the 'puppy' was taken care of, she had to hunt through Jenna's dirty clothes for three specific suits to take to the dry cleaners. The woman had piles and piles of dirty laundry. It looked like she had gone weeks without washing anything. But then again, her closet full of clean clothes was still overflowing. Perhaps she didn't realize she needed to wash before everything was dirty? The thought made Aubrey giggle a little. At least something about the day was making her smile.

Aubrey locked up Jenna's house and drove away. Watching the house grow smaller in her mirror, Aubrey decided she would have a house that big one day. She would put up with every one of the bullshit errands just to prove to herself, and to everyone else too, that she could do what it takes to succeed at something. What better proof of success than her own house. A house that beautiful.? A horse. She would make sure to have enough land to own a horse. And a trainer. If she owned a horse she would need to learn to ride. But it didn't matter. She would do it.

Lost in her thoughts about her hopeful future, Aubrey drove right passed the dry cleaners that Jenna wanted to use. Finding a place to make a U-turn took another ten minutes. When she finally got into the parking lot, the damn place was closed for lunch.

Aubrey looked at her watch, shocked that so much of the day was already gone. Instead of standing around and waiting for them to come back, she headed over to the store to pick up the tampons.

Henry was at the checkout. Fuck. Should she wander the store some and wait for him to leave, or just get in line and act as if his presence meant nothing to her? If she wandered, she wasted more time, and Jenna wouldn't be happy. But if she got in line and had to talk to him, she wouldn't be happy.

With a deep breath, she moved forward. She needed Jenna to be happy if she were ever going to get that damn horse.

She stood in line behind him holding the light pink box. Only then did she realize that she would rather wait on the horse if it meant keeping Henry from seeing her carrying tampons. They weren't even hers. How fucking embarrassing. If only she could just step back, slowly, quietly.

It would have worked if she hadn't tripped over a freaking basket someone left by the register instead of putting it away. Stupid lazy asshole. Aubrey fell backward and landed with a thud. Henry turned quickly, and as soon as his eyes landed on her, she could have sworn that they lit up just a bit.

She hoped it was because he was happy to see her and not because she was on her ass on the floor holding a stupid pink box of tampons.

"Let me help you," he said, holding out a hand. She considered telling him no, that she could get up just fine on her own. But then she thought how this might be the only time she would feel his hands on her body again—even if it were just a simple hand hold to get her up.

Aubrey placed her hand in his. He gave her a tug and wrapped his other hand around her back when she lost her footing for the second time. She was never that klutzy. Never. It had to be his fault.

"Thanks," she said, pulling her hand away. It was torture letting go of his touch. But she had to. He already took up too much of her mind. She had to find something about him to be irritated with, something to turn her off from him. She may have pulled her hand away, but she couldn't move away. And he couldn't stop looking at her.

Aubrey looked him up and down, looking for a flaw. He looked just as hot as he had the week prior. This time it was Teenage Mutant Ninja Turtle shoes. His sneakers had turtles on them. And he was rocking them. She couldn't even say his obsession with superheroes was a turn off. There was something about the sexy geek thing that made her smile.

"Sir?" the cashier asked, breaking the spell between them. Henry spun back around quickly and paid for his things, waiting calmly while she paid for the damn tampons. At least he had the decency to look away and pretend to not see what she was buying.

The two walked out of the store in silence. Aubrey wanted him to say something, anything, to break the awkwardness floating between them. She had no idea what sent them to a crashing halt the other night. But it didn't matter. She had to just get over it, over him. She didn't even know his last name, for crying out loud. There was no need to get all bent out of shape over someone who she didn't even know their last name.

"Aubrey, listen," he started.

"No, it's fine, really. You have a good day and thanks again for your help back there." Aubrey tried to walk away, but he reached out and grabbed her hand, running his thumb over her knuckles.

"Wait," he said. So she did. "Have dinner with me."

"I can't." She wanted to have him with dinner, but another date thing would just make it harder to walk away. It would be way too much like a date. Hell, he might even *consider* it a date. No, they were better off parting ways or jumping in the back seat of her car and going at it like bunnies before returning to work. That way they could have a smile in the middle of a bad day (at least her bad day), and they could get each other out of their systems. "But we could pick up where we left off the other night…"

Henry dropped her hand, and his soft expression turned hard.

"No, I don't think so. You have a good day." Then he walked off. Aubrey watched him go and was once again left feeling completely dejected.

~*~

Aubrey got back to the office in a fouler mood than when she left. She stalked into Jenna's office and placed the bag of tampons and the dry cleaning receipt on her very cluttered desk.

Aubrey laughed a little. She was gone for one afternoon, and Jenna's desk already looked like a war zone. She was lost without her. Maybe she will realize it and apologize for sending her out, or maybe buy her a coffee to thank her for everything she had done.

Probably not, but it was a nice thought.

Leaving the office, Aubrey noticed that most of the offices on her floor were empty. Glass walls were a wonderful thing at times. Bridgette came walking down the hall sipping her own drink. The bosses must be in a meeting that was expected to last a while.

"Hey, Bridgette, when did you get back?" she asked as her friend got closer. She hadn't seen her since the night at the club when she left with Henry.

"Last night. Where have you been all day? Jenna was going nuts trying to find stuff without you. She told Mike that you never called, but half the office saw you break a cup or something? I let him know you were here before, but I didn't know why you didn't check in with Jenna."

"Are you fucking kidding me? She sent me on errands. I had to walk her dog and buy her tampons. Why would she do that?" Aubrey had never felt so betrayed. What had she done so wrong? She always did her best and made Jenna look good. Wasn't that what she was supposed to do?

"I don't know what her issue is." Bridgette wouldn't look at her. She got like that when situations became intense. It wasn't anything she did or didn't do, but she hated any kind of conflict.

"She told Mike that I screwed up in New York. She didn't even have any meetings set up except the one that didn't even bother to show. I got us three meetings in a matter of thirty minutes, all for the same day. I kept Leslie from throwing us out the minute we walked in. Leslie even told me how great I was doing. But no, she threw me under the damn bus to make herself look better. And apparently, she was doing it again today. I don't know what the hell I did."

"I don't know, but it isn't right. I wouldn't say anything if you need your job, though. Before you, Jenna went through assistant after assistant. Just know that you won't be her PA forever." Bridgette leaned in and hugged her before heading back to her own desk.

Knowing she was on thin ice for a reason she didn't understand, she thought it best to be busy when Jenna returned from her meeting.

By the time the bosses were all walking back, Jenna's desk was clean and organized, there was a list of names and numbers that needed to be called by her personally, a stack of messages of clients that Aubrey had called for little things that needed to be clarified, and a cup of hot coffee sitting on the desk. She was really proud of herself.

"Aubrey, this looks wonderful, thank you. Now, here is the next list." Jenna handed her a paper, and then walked right passed her, sitting at her now clean desk.

"You're welcome," Aubrey replied before walking out the door. She had to keep it short and sweet, or she might not walk out with a job. The paper this time had a list of groceries, picking up the dry cleaning she dropped off, setting a doctor's appointment for Jenna, a vet appointment for the dog, and picking up a package from the post office.

At least there was no dog shit involved.

Aubrey made the appointments first since that could be done at her desk and right away. Then she called to check on the dry cleaning. No sense in going down there if they hadn't gotten to it yet. Once those were done, she grabbed her keys again and headed to the elevators.

"Aubrey, wait!" Mike yelled as he jogged down the hall. Aubrey stopped walking and watched as he continued to run toward her when he no longer had to. She started in his direction thinking it rude not to. He was her boss' boss, after all.

"Is there something I can get for you, Mike?"

"No, but there is something you can do for me. We have a huge meeting next week. I have asked that everyone push their travel meetings back a week. We need all hands on deck."

"Oh, Jenna didn't tell me. I will change the meeting dates right away. The errands can wait a few minutes."

"No, no. Jenna can do that, or you can do it later. Either way, that's not what I wanted to ask you. I need fresh eyes. This new client is some super genius high school kid who designed an entire video game in his basement and won some huge national award with it. Now he is shopping it around. We want it. Hell, we need it, to be honest. I need you to do some market research. Find the perfect target market and the data to support it. Think you can handle that?"

Aubrey couldn't believe what she was hearing. She wanted to jump up and down but thought that might be a little over the top. So instead she nodded vigorously with a big cheesy grin on her face. "Yes, yes, I can do that. Is there any way to get a summary of the game? Any information on the boy?"

"Ah, see, gender stereotyping. It was a girl who developed the game. And Jenna has all of that. I will let her know that I asked for you to help. If all goes well, maybe we can get you to do more of this… that is if you want."

"Yes, yes. I want. I mean, yes, I would very much like that. Thank you."

"You are welcome. Get whatever you have to done now, but first thing tomorrow morning, I want to see you working on this market research. We'll get a temp for Jenna."

Mike walked away, and Aubrey watched him disappear into his office. Bridgette turned and gave her a big smile with two thumbs up. Aubrey smiled and did a little happy dance right there in the hallway that lead to the elevators. With a smile on her face, she headed out to do the stupid errands knowing that the next day her real work would begin.

Chapter Six

Aubrey did her errands. She also did the third list that Jenna had waiting for her. And she did them all with a smile. Nothing was going to pull her down. She managed to impress the boss's boss enough for him to trust her with something as important as market research. Her plans on climbing the ranks in the company were working.

As the last light clicked off in the office, besides her own desk lamp, that is, Aubrey looked at the clock. It was almost seven thirty, and she was still working. If whatever temp they got to fill her shoes for the next few weeks couldn't decipher the notes or Jenna's schedule, then she would be pulling double duty to do the research and get the damn coffee.

All she wanted to do was dive into the bright red folder that sat on her desk next to her water bottle. It had all the new games information. But she knew if she opened it, all current work would cease to exist, and she would dive in. Aubrey stared at the folder for another moment before shaking her head and going back to work on scheduling for the next week.

After another hour had passed, Aubrey was finally done. She stacked all the papers, all with color coded tabs for each day and activity, on her desk with a note to her temp explaining everything. Then she stood, pushed in her chair, and grabbed the file that could be the key to her future and hugged it to her chest. With a big smile, she clicked off the light and headed out to her car.

She should celebrate. It would be the last night she would get to go out for at least a week, if not longer. It was a celebration kind of night. She did just get handed the key to a promotion, after all.

~*~

The dark bar was overflowing with people. Aubrey had no clue why a Monday night was so busy, but it didn't matter. The more people, the higher the energy level, and high energy and loud music were the best ways to unwind. High energy, loud music, and a strong drink were perfect for celebrating.

Aubrey weaved in and out and around a hundred bodies to get to the bar. Then she stopped dead in her tracks. Henry sat at the bar surrounded by women wearing half of what she considered decent. And that was saying something when she had clothing that left little to the imagination if the wind blew too hard.

No, she wouldn't let his presence, and the girls throwing themselves at him, deter her from celebrating. She wouldn't wallow in the past. He didn't want her, oh well. She could get anyone else in the entire place that she wanted.

Who wanted a geeky guy with a superhero fetish who couldn't even dance? Even if he were super hot and really fun to be around, it didn't matter. She was going to forget about him. Even if the t-shirt he had on did say 'ask me about my super powers' and fit him so snuggly it showed off his muscular frame, making her think that his super powers could very well be making her horny as hell just by sitting there. She was going to forget about Henry. Period. No ifs, ands, or buts. He was out of her mind. She wouldn't give him another thought.

Aubrey pushed her way to the bar and got the bartenders attention. He lifted up one finger, signaling her to hold on. She must be really off her game. First Henry, and then the bartender. Was she losing her touch? Maybe it was because she wasn't really dressed to be at the bar. She did come straight from work, but she knew she could pull off the sexy secretary look just fine if she undid the top two buttons of her blouse. She wore skirts most days anyway, and heels were her addiction. She had on a white blouse, black pencil skirt, and bright red heels that matched her necklace.

Popping her buttons on her blouse, she cleared her throat. The bartender looked in her direction and his eyes widened. She took that moment to reach up and free her long dark hair from her bun. It spilled over her shoulders in waves, and she smiled at him, batting her lashes. She may be cliché, but she knew it. She owned it. Hell, why would she do anything different when it worked?

The bartender then gave the hold on finger to the half dressed woman in front of him, who went back to hanging all over Henry (not that she cared) and moved directly in front of her. He was definitely cute. But she wasn't into bartenders. At least not the ones at her usual places. It made things too awkward after the fact. She may be a barfly, but she wasn't a bartender floozy.

"What can I get you tonight?" he asked, already pulling a glass from the bar.

"Tonight's a celebration, so let's go with a long island."

"What are you celebrating, gorgeous?" His hands moved quickly as he mixed her drink, the alcohol flowing from the bottles at the same time as the mixers. He gave her an extra shot or two, whether he realized it or not, his pour was strong.

"A possible promotion at work. I do this assignment well, and I won't be getting anyone's coffee anymore." Aubrey took the drink and handed over her credit card. It was an open tab kind of night.

"Sounds like the perfect night to celebrate, but doing it alone isn't fun."

Aubrey took a drink and sure enough, it was strong. The alcohol burned going down, heating her through to her stomach. She looked up and smiled at the bartender. "Don't worry. I'm sure I won't be alone for long."

Prickles covered the back of her neck, making her feel as if she were being watched. She knew it was Henry. She just knew it. Ignoring the impulse to turn in his direction, she grabbed her drink and walked off. She wouldn't look back. She wouldn't.

Aubrey found a table that was small and empty, and surrounded by a group of people. The way it was placed in the room kept her hidden from Henry's view, but if the stupid guy in front of her would just step to the right half a step, she could sneak a peek at him and his gaggle of girls.

Stupid girls.

The guy in front of her moved. She saw Henry. He had angled himself so he could see her, too. She locked eyes with him from across the bar, and even when people walked between them, she never looked away, and neither did he.

She refused to move. She wouldn't chase him. But she found that the farther into her drink she got, the less she remembered why she wasn't pursuing this nearly perfect man. Who cared that he turned her down? That just made it more fun. She should wear him down. She could just picture what he looked like under those clothes, what his hands would feel like rubbing against her skin, what his hot mouth…

She didn't finish her thought. She couldn't, because if she did, she may combust into an orgasmic puddle of goo on the bar floor. Aubrey stood and marched across the bar. Henry smiled at her as she approached, and the stupid girls glared at her. Screw them.

When she stood directly in front of Henry, she reached out and took his hand, ignoring the comments being spewed by the half dressed women around them, and led him away. She didn't speak to him, or respond to the girls. She just took what she wanted.

And she wanted Henry.

Once again she found herself dancing on Henry, but that was fine. She managed to move and rub up against him in ways that had him start exploring her body with his hands. Finally, they landed on her hips, his thumbs kneading into her ass, pulling her tightly against his hardening length,

Aubrey stood straight, lifting her arms above her head to wrap around his neck as she swayed back and forth. When his hot breath caressed the soft skin of her neck, she shivered in delight. When her earlobe was encased in the wet warmth of his mouth, the throbbing between her legs began. When his teeth bit down, she knew she had lost all control.

As soon as he released her earlobe from his teeth, Aubrey whipped around, pressing her body tightly to his, her hands wound into his hair, and she crushed her lips to his. She was done being rejected. She was done walking away from this man a hot horny mess.

Henry did not disappoint. He responded with more fervor than she ever thought he would. His lips parted over hers, and he dipped his tongue into her eagerly awaiting mouth. He massaged her tongue with his own, and then would pull back to softly kiss her and nip at her lips, and then deepen it once again. She had never been kissed that way before, and it was incredible.

When they parted, the two just stared into one another's eyes for a moment. Aubrey could see so much emotion and desire in his. He wanted her. She knew he did. But would he follow through or would he send her on her way like he already has too many times for her liking.

When Henry slid his hands from her hips, she thought for sure the night was coming to a crashing halt. But then he took her hand in his, leading her out of the bar and toward what she could only assume was his car.

When a man exited the driver's seat and opened the back door, she looked at the Henry in question. He just shook his head and motioned for her to get in. She did.

Henry slid in after her, and that was when she noticed that the windows were all tinted, and there was a privacy glass separating the driver from the back seat. Whoever Henry really was, he was much more than Hot Geeky Guy, who she couldn't get off her mind.

"Can he see or hear us?" she asked in a breathy voice.

"Not unless we push the button."

"Don't push it."

Aubrey moved to straddle Henry and slowly worked her hips, grinding her pulsating pussy against his lap. The friction did nothing to help the need that was growing between her legs. She needed more.

Henry ran his hands up her thighs and under her skirt, bunching it at her waist. Aubrey leaned down to kiss him, letting her mouth explore his. When his hands began guiding her movements, pulling her closer to him, her tongue grew frantic. She needed to feel his skin against her own. She pulled back and unbuttoned her top, revealing her lace covered breasts to him. His eyes glowed with anticipation as he reached up, freeing them from her bra. Aubrey watched as Henry leaned in and took her hard nipple into his mouth.

She moaned at the contact and jerked her hips, and he bit down then sucked at her nipple, soothing the sting from his teeth. She could feel how hard he was beneath her. She didn't want him under her—she wanted him in her.

When he let go of her nipple, she moved herself to the floorboard between his legs and undid his Spiderman belt and unbuttoned his jeans. Henry lifted his hips slightly, and she gave his jeans a tug, exposing his large cock in one swift move.

Aubrey wrapped her hands around him and began to pump up and down. Then she leaned forward and took him in her mouth. She ran her tongue around the head of his dick and then sucked it into her mouth. She moved back to his head and repeated her movements, all the while pumping the base of him that she couldn't get to fit in her mouth. He groaned in approval and that pleased Aubrey. She wanted to make him feel good. She wanted him to fall apart, and she wanted to see him cum.

Aubrey looked up, without stopping her ministrations, to see his head thrown back and a smile on his lips. She worked harder, working him, humming around his member, and sliding her hands up and down his length. When he looked to her, and their eyes caught, she felt a flutter in her stomach. His gaze held her captivated. He reached out and moved a stray hair from her face and pulled himself from her mouth. She wanted to protest, but he pulled her to the seat next to him and laid her down on the seat.

Slowly, his hands traced up from her ankle to circle the soft skin behind her knee. The heat his hands left in their wake made her skin feel as if it were being scorched, even through her pantyhose. From her knee, he slowly, tortuously, moved up her thighs, running his thumb over her covered slit and up to the top of her pantyhose. Hooking his fingers in, he pulled them off her. Then he retraced the pattern, only this time he used his mouth. Each fiery kiss ignited something in her, more than sheer desire, but she pushed it away. She wanted to stay in the moment, the passionate moment where his lips and tongue explored every inch of her.

When his warm breath ghosted across her pussy lips, she shivered. Her skin erupted in goose bumps and she waited, and waited, and waited to feel the warmth of his mouth against her, in her.

She lost all patience. When she looked down at him between her legs, he was smiling at her. Not the coy, we are about to do it grin that so many men get, but a full on smile. He was waiting to see what she would do. She gave him a smile of her own, grabbed two fists full of hair, and placed his face exactly where she needed him.

His tongue traced her slit, once, twice, and a third time. Her hips jerked up to him, begging for more. She held tightly to his hair and tugged as he nipped at her lips, then her thigh. She yanked his hair, pulling him back to her center. She could feel his chuckle against her, and she looked down, wondering what he found so funny.

He kissed her softly then looked up into her eyes, and said, "I like to have fun when I have sex. Playing makes it more fun. And more memorable. You won't ever forget this night."

He didn't give her a chance to respond. He dove in, licking and sucking on her clit in a rhythm that sent her body into overdrive. He was right—she would never forget the amazing job he was doing licking her pussy. She could feel the tension building in her, her muscles beginning to tighten from her core outward. Aubrey cried out as every muscle in her body began to spasm as she fell over the edge of orgasmic bliss.

As she lay there catching her breath, she could hear rustling of clothes and a crinkle of plastic. Aubrey pulled herself up to a sitting position and watched as he rolled a condom on his long length. Wanting to give him the release she just received, she climbed back on top of him, sinking down, taking his entire length inside of her.

They both moaned as he filled her. She rocked her hips back and forth, and then lifted herself and sank back down, over and over. Henry's mouth found her bouncing tits and sucked them in, limiting her movements, but neither cared. It felt fucking amazing. When he released her, she leaned back and continued to rock herself faster and faster. His hands gripped her hips, and then slipped into the crease of her legs. He reached his thumb out and began rubbing circles on her clit as she rode him.

Henry pulled his hands back, grabbed her around her waist, and lifted her off him. Aubrey knelt on the seat beside him, watching to see what he would do next. She didn't care how he wanted it as long as his cock was inside of her, fast and hard.

Aubrey took that moment to appreciate him in all his naked glory. She was right—he was toned and muscular, but not big and bulky. He had the perfect washboard abs with the V that lead to his glorious cock surrounded by blonde curls. He was perfect.

"Flip over for me," Henry's husky and lust-filled voice broke her from her trance. She did what he asked, lifting her hips, putting her ass on display for him. His hands traced down her spine and rounded her ass around to her hot center. A single finger dipped between her folds, caressing her, spreading her wetness. She looked over her shoulder and watched as he guided his dick to her center, then felt him push in, filling her again. With every stroke, his cock did more to her than she ever knew possible, filling her, stretching her, pushing her closer and closer to the edge for the second time. She began thrusting herself back with every push forward he made, causing him to go deeper and harder. When his movements became sporadic and rapid, she knew he was almost there. So was she. She was so close she thought if she didn't finish she might combust.

When his hand wrapped around her and dipped down, she fell apart. His fingers circling her clit, and his dick pounding into her from behind, sent her into oblivion. Her body convulsed as she cried out. When Henry stopped moving and moaned deep and gravelly, she knew that he too had reached his edge and fallen over.

The two collapsed onto the seat and just laughed when they realized that the car had stopped moving. She really hoped that the windows were as sound proof as Henry seemed to think they were.

"If I asked you to come back to my place for the night, would you?" Henry asked, and then kissed her shoulder.

"I can't. I have to work in the morning. I actually might be getting a promotion. That is, if I kick ass at this market research. Going from a personal assistant to a market researcher would be a huge jump on the career train track, ya know?"

"I do. What kind of market research?"

"I know it sounds corny, but video games. I was never really into them as a kid, and now I work for one of the largest companies trying to sell them. Anyway, my boss's boss gave me the assignment. Some kid came up with some new game, and I need to find the target market for it. Maybe come up with a way to reach them, too."

Aubrey didn't realize until it was too late that she was opening up, letting him in. She hadn't lain in a man's arms after sex and just talked since the fuck up that was her ex-boyfriend. She moved to sit up and started dressing. If Henry were upset by it, she didn't notice. She kept her back to him while she covered herself. If she looked back at him and saw that he didn't want her to move just yet, she might give in. And that she couldn't afford to do.

"That is a really big deal, what firm do you work for?"

"Viola."

"Oh, good. I mean, that's a really good company." There was something about his voice that made her wonder what was going through his head. Was he bothered by her pulling away? Did it surprise him that she was putting her career first? Did he not think she was capable of market research?

"What do you mean, *oh, good?*"

"I just mean that it's a good company. That's all. Do you want me to take you home?"

"Back to the bar if we could. My car is there."

"Sure thing." Henry then pressed a button on his door that made a little buzzing sound, and the driver answered as if it were a phone.

"Hello, sir. What can I do for you?"

"Back to the bar, please. This lovely lady needs her car."

"Right away, sir."

Aubrey wanted to question him about everything. The car, the driver, being called sir, but she had a feeling he was glad she didn't. Maybe he didn't want to talk about work or money for a reason. She just hoped he wasn't some mob guy in a geeky undercover thing. Did those even exist? She didn't know, but she really hoped not.

The car pulled back into the bar parking lot much too soon for her liking. And that scared her. When the door was opened, and Henry helped her out, just holding his hand made her smile. Or it could have been the post orgasmic euphoria running through her. Either way, he was responsible.

With a kiss goodnight to rival all others, Aubrey and Henry said goodbye. She could feel him watching her as she walked away, and she fought the urge to look back at him. She needed to keep her distance. It didn't matter that he was sweet and funny and goofy and incredibly good at making her scream in unmatched pleasure. What mattered was staying focused on the market research. That was her future. Not some guy she met in a bar whose last name she didn't even know. Even if he made her feel things she hadn't felt in a long time. No, she would not focus on Henry anymore. She had gotten what she wanted. It was time to move on, just like every other guy. Only Henry wasn't every other guy.

When she reached her car, she couldn't help herself. She looked back to where he had kissed her goodnight. He was still standing there, watching her. Without a wave or any acknowledgement of his presence, she climbed in her car. She felt like a complete bitch.

Aubrey screamed in frustration once she had completely closed her car door. No need to scare anyone over her own drama that she had created. She had no one to blame but herself... and maybe Henry's parents since they made the perfect man. How was she supposed to stick to her guns when the perfect man was pursuing her?

She turned the key in the ignition and put the car in drive. As she left the parking lot, she figured it out.

The only way to stick to her plan of career before a man was to avoid him altogether.

Henry Hot Geeky Superhero Guy was not going to see her again. She would avoid him at all costs, and eventually, they would both be able to forget the other.

Chapter Seven

Aubrey poured over her notes again and again over the next few days. This girl was sixteen and wrote a game code so amazing that it put some seasoned gamer veterans to shame. Aubrey was never one to really get into video games, but there was a sample game in the folder. She popped the disc into the computer to check it out.

The whole game world was based on ancient Greek mythology. The male characters were scantily clad in their togas, and the women were actually well proportioned and mostly covered. She had to laugh at the complete one eighty this game was pulling on the entertainment world in general.

It wasn't until Aubrey noticed the clock clicking over to seven thirty that she realized how immersive the game could be. She had been playing for two hours. It was more than puzzles, more than quests, and more than action. It had it all, and a compelling storyline to go with it. If all she had were a sample, she couldn't wait to get her hands on the full version.

Just by reading the file, and playing the game, Aubrey knew that the target market was going to be female. She just had to figure out the perfect age range. She found that nine times out of ten, the best way to get that information was to ask.

Aubrey printed off a few images from the game as well as a short summary and packed up. She was going to go to all the local malls, the business district, and restaurant row, and she would ask any woman she passed. She also intended to ask the men, just to prove her thoughts were accurate.

It wasn't until she was driving down the road heading to the mall that she realized where exactly she was. The diner that Henry took her too was on that street. Thinking of Henry made her smile and her heart ache at the same time. She took a sharp right to find a detour. No reminders. No thinking. No feelings.

It needed to be that simple. Too bad it wasn't. It's not as if she was in love with the guy, but Aubrey knew, if given the chance, she could be. Henry was the type of man she would fall head over heels for, and then do something to fuck it up, which would send him running and screaming. She sucked at relationships.

Most men were content with the whole fuck buddy thing. Not Henry. Why did he have to actually care? Aubrey turned her radio on and turned the volume up until she could literally feel the vibrations from the bass in her seat. If the memories insisted on invading her brain, she would wash them away with a good solid music session.

~*~

It took almost the entire week for Aubrey to actually think of something that she wanted to present to Mike. He had approached her on a few occasions asking questions about her progress, and when she didn't have answers for him, she felt like a failure, and he looked so disappointed. It wasn't that she didn't know the demographic, because she did. It was that she hadn't compiled the exact numbers to prove her theory was accurate. He wouldn't care about a hunch. He would care what the numbers said. The day before, he didn't ask her. He gave her a meeting time and told her to bring everything she had.

Aubrey stood outside Mike's door for almost five minutes, just staring at it. This was it. Do or die. Either she was made for the business or she wasn't. She knew that she was lucky to have the opportunity, but she was terrified that she would fuck it all up and lose everything. The stupid temp girl they got to fill in for Jenna was actually doing well. She could easily be her replacement.

She was never going to get out of that stupid attic. She was going to have to live with her parents and little brother forever. Her brother would move out before her. This was pointless. Aubrey looked down at the file in her hands. She worked hard on it. She put everything she had into the research and the ideas she came up with to help market it. She even put together a grass roots plan that has proven to work in other media industries. What if it weren't as good as she thought it was when she finished the night before? What if she weren't as good as she thought?

The door swung open, startling Aubrey. Mike stood before her with a quizzical look on his face. "Well, are you coming in or not?"

"Yes. I mean, I am. Sorry." She knew she was rambling, but there was little she could do to stop it. Mike stepped back, holding out an arm, welcoming her in. She had been in his office many times before, but it was usually to deliver a fax or a coffee, not a presentation.

"Aubrey, I need you to be straight with me. Do you have anything?" Mike looked worried. She hadn't meant to give him the impression she wasn't working on anything all week, but she didn't want to say one thing and be wrong and have to correct herself later.

"I do. I have a lot, actually. I don't know if it's what you were expecting, but I worked really hard on it and—"

"Take a breath. I'm sure it's fine. Let me see the file."

Aubrey did as he said. She took a deep breath, and with shaky and not quite steady hands, she handed over the file. She sat in the chair, but she was far from comfortable. Mike thumbed through her notes. Every now and then he would 'hmmm' or 'huh'. Sometimes he would mark something down. But he didn't say a word to her for the ten minutes it took him to browse everything she had spent the last week working on.

"Okay, tell me your findings."

"But, you just read them all."

"I know that, but I want to hear your pitch. I want to hear how you would explain it to the client, and how you would sell it."

"Oh." She hadn't prepared for that. She began to fidget and look anywhere but at Mike.

"Aubrey, this is really good. All of it. But you have to be able to sell it. You have to be confident in your work, in yourself, and in this company. You have all these numbers and graphs and definitions in here that are all very good research. But what makes us the best company to sell it? Why should this genius girl trust our company to take her computer program and turn it into a game for all platforms? Why are we the best fit for her? Did you look at her personal bio at all or just the game?"

"The game. I can do better. I can do a cram session on the girl and get you everything before the meeting tomorrow. I promise I can do this. I'm sorry, please, give me another chance." Every self-doubt that had ever crossed her mind rushed to the surface. She screwed up. She wasn't good enough. She wasn't smart enough. She wasn't enough.

"Slow down, what you have done is really good. You have real potential, Aubrey. I want you to come to the pitch tomorrow. You are going to tell them your ideas on how to get this game in front of the right people. Just finish the file. And I will see you first thing in the morning at Baker and Baker to pitch."

"Baker and Baker? The lawyer's building? Why isn't she coming here?"

"Because apparently we are in a serious competition for the business, and the girl's mother thought it best to be at their lawyer's office for his help andneutral ground. Is it a pain? Yes. Is it normal for people who don't know how to read a contract? Yes to that too."

Mike handed the file back to Aubrey before turning to his computer screen. She had been dismissed. Standing, she quickly thanked him again for the opportunity, and slipped out the door. If she were going to pull off this presentation, she needed to focus.

Sitting at her temporary desk in a little office just outside of Jenna's office, she read about the designer of the game over and over. There had to be some clue in there to connect with the girl, besides her game. She was a teenager. She was an artist and had won a few local awards for it, and she was really into computers and coding. None of that had any real meaning to Aubrey. She needed more. She wanted to know her favorite band, shows, foods, places to visit. Something that she could use to establish a friendly atmosphere before they started talking business.

Then she saw it. A photo of the girl wearing a headband. The same headband that was sitting on her own dresser at home. They both liked music. She could work with that.

~*~

A rapid tap tap tap echoed through the well decorated hallway. Aubrey looked around at Jenna, Mike, and a few other higher ups she didn't really know all that well who stared back at her.

It wasn't until then that she realized the tapping came from her. Her leg was bouncing a mile a minute and her high heel were hitting the ground. She slowed her leg to a stop and gave them all a week smile. She wanted to throw up.

Just behind the doors that stood a mere thirty feet away were the clients. And the competition. When they arrived, they had been told the earlier meeting was running late and to have a seat. Aubrey couldn't help but wonder who was in there. It could be any number of companies in there pitching. Did any of them have the same ideas she had? Was the meeting running late because they loved the idea so much that no matter what Viola presented, it was a waste of time? Mike and Jenna sat in their chairs, reading notes or something, but completely calm. Aubrey had no idea how they managed to keep calm.

A creaking noise sounded through the hall, and all eyes landed on the doors to see who came out and what their expressions were. A dozen men walked out, none of which showed anything other than boredom, giving Aubrey a bit of hope.

"Great. They've been with Maximus. And not just his minions. Look," Jenna said and gave a little head nod in the direction of a man facing the other way, shaking hands with who Aubrey thought was a Barker. The thought that Maximus had been in before them was like a lead balloon. All the hope she had just acquired sank to the ground in a rush.

Then he turned around, and all air escaped her. Henry stood there in a fancy suit, his hair combed and gelled down, and not a single superhero reference on his clothing. Who was this man?

Henry finally saw her standing there. His whole being sort of deflated and he took a step toward her. Aubrey shook her head. No, she couldn't handle him at that moment. She had to give a presentation that would shoot whatever the hell he did in there out of the water.

But he didn't stop. He kept coming, and there was nowhere for her to go. She couldn't leave, yet she really didn't want to stay. She didn't want to hear him apologize for lying to her. She didn't want to hear him tell her it was fun and so long (even if that's all she had been trying to convince herself of for weeks), and she really didn't want her bosses to know she slept with the enemy.

"Aubrey, listen—" Henry started. His voice was just as deep and smooth as ever, and her body instantly reacted to it, craving him. But her heart, the traitorous stupid thing it was, was aching at the thought that it was all a game to him.

"No, Henry. I need to go in there and give a presentation. But you already knew that, didn't you." Aubrey did walk away that time, but only because Mike and Jenna were already at the door with Mr. Baker heading in. She pushed passed Henry and toward the board room.

"Wait," she heard him say as she crossed over the threshold. Mr. Baker closed the door behind him and put up a much needed wall between her and Henry. All eyes from her company were on here, Jenna in a much more accusatory way then the rest. Jenna looked at her with squinted eyes and a pucker to her lips. Aubrey knew she didn't tell Henry anything that would hurt their own campaign, but did he know about it before she opened her big fat post coital mouth?

"Let's get started, shall we? This is Ms. Becca Stine, and this is her mother, Gloria Stine. Ms. Stine has invited you here to hear why she should go with Viola instead of any other gaming company." Mr. Baker sat down after the introductions were made, at least for his clients. It was time to wow them.

Mike stood and gave his presentation on Viola as a company. He told Becca about the community work Viola did, about the long history in the gaming world, and about some break out gaming hits which they were responsible for marketing.

"Hey, what the hell was that out there?"" Jenna leaned over and whispered to her. Aubrey didn't want to think about Henry. She wanted to pay attention to the meeting. This was her first time where she got to sit at the table instead of taking notes on a notepad leaning against the wall in the back of the room.

"Not now," she whispered back. Aubrey watched Becca and her mother. She wanted to see their reactions to everything Mike was saying. From the looks of it, neither was very impressed.

"Yes now—I need some kind of ammunition against Maximus, and apparently, you know the man himself."

"No. Would you stop talking so I can listen, please?" Aubrey's patience was waning. Jenna huffed and sat back in her chair, crossing her arms. Aubrey couldn't help but think how unprofessional she was being. Becca seemed to take note of Jenna's attitude, and even made sure her mother noticed, as well. She would have to work fast if she wanted a chance to give her presentation. She really hoped she hit the nail on the head with the marketing plan.

"I'm going to turn the floor over to our market researcher now to give you an idea of where we would like to go with your product." Mike smiled at her and gave her an encouraging nod before sitting down.

Aubrey took a deep breath and stood, walking over to the computer that controlled the room's projector screen. She pressed a button and the title of the game came up.

"Hi, there. I'm Aubrey, and I have to be honest with you, I'm not much of a game person. I have been working at Viola as an assistant for three years and just have a real knack for numbers. I can look at charts and lists and pick out the best algorithms in them. For most people, that is the perfect combination for market research.

"But I didn't want to just do that with you. When I heard your story, and then turned on Artimas Moon, I knew that just numbers weren't enough."

Aubrey clicked through some screen shots she took while playing. It showed her female character hunting, fighting, and finally saving a human. "With a character like Artimas, she had to have a special kind of marketing. You need a special kind of marketing."

"What do you mean me?" Becca asked, being engaged for the first time.

"I mean, we need to market you as much as the game. We need you to be central in everything. This was your project. I don't want you to give it to a company who will just use the basic plot line and change everything. You created strong female characters. You even made them wear clothes, which is becoming rare in video games aimed at a more mature market. You are sure to design more games in the future, and with this one? This is a game that needs to be marketed to girls.

"I want to put together a list of your favorite bands, songs of female empowerment, and instrumentals all performed by female artists to do the soundtrack for the game. I want to start a grass roots movement in your town of the girls who know you and have played the game to help get the word out. I want to send actors and actresses around to malls and game stores in costume to act out scenes from your game, and I want them to be cute enough to get all the girls attention."

Becca was smiling from ear to ear as she listened to Jenna talk. She knew she was on a role when her mother spoke up, bursting her figurative bubble.

"How much?"

"Excuse me?"

"How much are you going to pay my daughter for her game? She has a very expensive college waiting for her."

"Well, ma'am, that isn't my department." Aubrey looked back to Jenna quickly who rolled her eyes and stood up.

"Ladies, the money can be negotiated. Everything that Aubrey mentioned is a good idea. It is proven that when customers connect with a product or brand on another level, they buy more. We want to make Becca the brand. She is the reason we are all here. Girl power, and all that."

"I understand that. But we still need to know she will be taken care of. We have received some very generous offers today."

Aubrey knew she shouldn't speak up without first talking to Mike, but she didn't want to lose the contract. "What if we can offer her a job after high school? A part time entry level position while she is in college."

Mike snapped his eyes to her, and she saw the look he was sending her. They didn't have the ability to do that without the human resource department getting involved. But Aubrey couldn't think of a single reason they would turn her down.

"In addition to the lump sum for the rights to her game?" Mrs. Stine asked. Becca was practically bouncing in her seat, and Aubrey caught sight of her hitting her mom's leg over and over. Becca wanted the deal. Hell, she knew Becca wanted it before her mother started talking numbers.

"Yes, in addition to," Jenna said. She finally took note of the situation. She wasn't going to reprimand Aubrey just yet. She knew it would be coming, but if they signed Becca Stine, it would be worth it.

"What if she can only work five hours a week because of school, or what if she needs twenty?"

"That will have to be worked out with the department she starts in. But at Viola, we are very flexible with college students. We understand the importance of going to class. We even have a program that gives bonuses to employees who make the dean's list at their respective colleges."

"YES! I want to go with you!" Becca called out, standing from the table. Aubrey smiled brightly at her and thought the deal was done. She was wrong.

"No, we need to know what they are offering first." Her mother grabbed her arm and pulled her back down to a sitting position.

"Jenna, would you please put Mrs. Stine's mind at ease and show her the contract that we will amend to include the employment should you sign," Mike said. When Aubrey looked at him, he looked defeated, as if he knew something she didn't. Was she reading the situation wrong? The girl wanted Viola.

"I'm sorry, but we can not agree to anything right now. We need to compare all the offers, and we will get back to you next week." Mrs. Stine stood and walked to the door to open it. "You all have a great day."

They were being dismissed. The worst part? As they walked out dejected and wondering where they went wrong, Henry stood there waiting for her.

Chapter Eight

"Go away, Henry." Aubrey walked passed him with her colleagues, who were all watching the interaction with rapt attention.

"Not without talking to you first. Just hear me out. Please." He kept up with her, stride for stride, no matter how fast she tried to walk.

"No. There is nothing to explain. You should have told me who you were."

Aubrey pushed the door open and walked out. She could hear him cursing from behind her, but she didn't look back. Not for Henry, and not for either Jenna or Mike, who were both calling her name. She had to be alone. Her embarrassment was no one's business but her own.

The sky that had been completely clear when she entered the building was now filled with clouds. She could feel a mist in the air and hoped to make it to her car before the sky opened up.

She didn't. The water poured down on top of her, soaking her straight through to her skin in a matter of minutes. Not caring how she looked any longer, she kicked off her shoes, grabbed them in one hand, and ran to her car.

Once locked inside, she stared out the window through the waves of water that were flowing down the glass, and cried.

How could she let herself get so caught up in a man again? How could she let his deception hurt her? How could she let him in so much so that she jeopardized the first, and probably last, chance she had at becoming more than Jenna's assistant?

That was it. She was done. Henry was a thing of the past, and she would pick herself up and move on just like every other time. He would not be the reason she stopped moving forward. If that girl and her mother couldn't see that a career opportunity was better than a lump sum all at once, then they aren't nearly as smart as they were made out to be.

Aubrey wiped her eyes and turned her car on. With determination in her eyes, she left the parking lot and headed back to the office.

~*~

Going straight to the office wasn't her best idea. Soaking wet clothing are not the most comfortable things to wear while trying to research how best to win the Stines over. Aubrey was desperate to find something about Maximus to show to them to prove that money wasn't everything. It had to be more than the obvious. Anyone in the gaming industry, or who was interested in it like Becca was, would know that Viola was the largest and oldest company around.

They would already know the titles under their belts and the backing they received from other industries. But Maximus was this shiny new toy everyone wanted to check out and play with for the past few years, effectively cutting into Viola's profits, cutting into all the other companies' profits, too.

Maybe Henry made a habit of seducing women with his 'I'm not that kind of guy' ways. Maybe he had a sordid past she could dig up. Maybe if she Googled his name…

No. This wasn't about Henry. She was done with him. Done, done, done.

But when she Googled Maximus industries, it became a little impossible to ignore him. His beautiful eyes stared back at her, picture after picture, article after article. The company was squeaky fucking clean.

Maybe she had to look more into Henry Maximus. Not that she wanted to. She absolutely didn't want to.

Another quick search brought up his biography. Surely he had some kind of a sordid past.

Only, he didn't. He grew up in her town, went to her high school, graduated the year before her. *Holy shit, they went to school together.*

That was when she really began to search for anything she could find on Henry Maximus. Research for work completely forgotten, she was looking for high school photos. Surely, she would remember him. He was fucking hot as hell, and with those moves he had, every girl would have been talking about him. But then again, she thought, there is no way Henry was a jock. She pretty much stuck to the football team when it came to boyfriends. Yes, she was the stereotypical cheerleader. Hot, popular, and dated the football players.

Thinking back on it, she kind of disgusted herself. Maybe if she tried harder then, actually paid attention to anything other than her friends or boyfriends, she wouldn't have started her 'grown-up' life completely behind the curve.

His senior picture popped up, or what they claimed to be his senior picture, and she recognized it immediately. Henry was the kid that they all teased. Well, she never teased him, but she didn't talk to him either. She just ignored him. She couldn't bring herself to actually be that mean to someone, but she also couldn't bring herself to jeopardize her standing and let anyone see her being nice to the outcasts, either. She wasn't sure what was worse, doing the teasing or knowing its wrong and doing nothing about it.

Could Henry have realized who she was to begin with? Was he trying to prove something? But why should it matter? She didn't want a relationship. She wanted a fun night, and she got it. But it kind of stung like a bitch to know she was some sort of conquest, some sort of game.

Aubrey couldn't look at the stupid computer screen anymore. She shoved away from her desk and made a plan. She would go home and put on her hottest club outfit she owned. Then she would drive an hour back into the city, and she would make sure that Henry saw her with someone else.

The thought of him knowing he hurt her sucked. He probably did it on purpose, that bastard. So what if he were a complete loser in high school? That wasn't her fault. So he made a life for himself, a billionaire type life. Was he having fun shoving it in her face that she only became an assistant without a degree?

But if that were true, he probably would have mentioned the money thing. But it didn't matter. He had to have known who she was, and the minute he knew she worked for Viola, he should have been honest with her. He hid who he was from her. He was an ass.

The drive home was filled with loud music and a speedometer that was well above sixty-five. Aubrey parked the car and stormed into her house, not bothering to speak to anyone. Her brother had yet to get over his little tantrum, and her parents were sitting at the dining room table eating dinner. Food could wait. She had a man to find and another to prove to that she wasn't affected by him in the least.

Stomping up the stairs to the attic, Aubrey stopped mid way. She heard the creak of the bottom step behind her. Slowly, she turned around to see her brother at the bottom looking up at her with those stupid sad eyes he always got when he really needed to talk. Not because he was pissed off, but because he was hurting over something.

The anger faded quickly and was replaced by concern for him. She just gave him a half smile and nodded up toward her room.

"Come on, Ben." Aubrey continued climbing the stairs knowing her brother would follow. He had come around as he always does. She just wished he didn't have to be so upset to do so.

Opening the door, she let him in where he promptly kicked off his shoes and flopped on her bed. Since her clothing was still wet, she began shuffling through her drawers and found her outfit for the night. She sat it down on the chair next to the stairs and sat on the floor with her knees tucked to her chest and waited for Ben to start talking.

"I don't know what to do."

"Okay," she said slowly as she watched her brother's eyes glass over. A tear fell but was wiped away quickly. "You have to tell me what's going on."

"Mackenna is pregnant." Ben's head fell into his hands as his shoulders shook. Aubrey couldn't believe what she was hearing, but she couldn't let Ben cry without some kind of comfort. It was rare for her to see him this way. She could only think of a couple times he showed this much emotion since he was about ten or so. She stood and sat next to him on the bed, wet clothes and all, and took her little brother into her arms. Her stupid, stupid brother who had just made the biggest mistake of his life.

"Have you told Mom and Dad?"

"No."

"Has she told her parents?"

"Not yet."

"What do you want?"

"I don't know."

"Well, little brother, I think it's time you figured that out. You can't be a kid anymore. You have to grow up."

Aubrey held her little brother in her arms for over an hour. He was going to need her more than ever. Her baby brother, in all of his fifteen years, was about to be a father.

"Aubrey?" he whispered, trying to mask his tears.

"Yeah?"

"Think you could take me over to Mackenna's? She shouldn't have to tell her parents alone."

"Yeah, I can take you over there on my way back into the city. Give me twenty minutes to get dressed, and I will drop you off. You call me if you need anything, and I will come straight back. Okay?"

"Yeah, okay. Thanks." Ben got up and left her room. All Aubrey could do was sit there and stare at the door. What the hell was he going to do? Should she still go to the bar? Or should she wait for Ben at the house? But if she were home, how could she keep that kind of information from their parents? No, she had to leave, so that way he would be the one to tell them. She would make sure he told them soon, like the next day if he hadn't managed to tell them before she got home, but it wasn't her news to tell. He came to her, so she had to respect that and give him the chance to do the right thing.

Aubrey slipped into her little red dress that flowed like waves down her body. It was short and cleavage-baring, but it wasn't tight anywhere but the bodice. When she spun while dancing, it sort of belled out, allowing her freedom of movement. Pairing it with a pair of black pumps, and she was out the door.

"You ready, Ben?" she called as she walked down the stairs.

That's when she heard it. The arguing. Low and angry, but definitely arguing.

"Benjamin, you are grounded or don't you remember that? Your girlfriend can see you tomorrow at school. It's nine at night, and you think you are going out? Are you crazy? You are fifteen years old!"

"I am going. She needs me. Just let me go." Ben's voice was steady. He wasn't yelling, or even being argumentative, but their parents were not having it. Aubrey stood in the doorway to the living room, watching. Should she say something or let Ben handle it? He was right that he needed to go, but their mom and dad didn't know that.

"Absolutely not. Go upstairs, right now," their father said.

"Dad, come on, please just trust me on this."

"HA! Trust you? What have you done to show us you can be trusted? Ever since you started dating that girl you have been nothing but a little hellion. You don't listen, you stay out all night, and your grades are falling. Do you have any idea how hard it is to get your GPA back up? Do you plan on going to college or just living here the rest of your life?"

That stung. Aubrey knew her father wasn't talking to her, but he was thinking about it when he said that. Did her brother want to be a failure like her? Of course not, and she didn't want that for him either.

"I'm leaving," Ben said then strolled passed her. Her parents were hot on his trail, but she put her hand to her father's chest. She didn't know what she was doing until it was too late, but she had stepped in. Again.

"Dad, let him go. You have no idea what's going on. Just let him go. He is trying to do the right thing and right now, in this instance, the right thing isn't listening to you. Please, just trust me on this, even if you can't trust him."

"He is fifteen years old. The right thing is always listening to me. What the hell is going on, Aubrey?"

"It's not my place to tell you, but I will make sure he does, okay?"

"Not okay. Tell me."

"Bye, Dad. I'll be home later. And so will Ben."

She followed the path that Ben set and found him in her car, staring out the window into nothingness. Her parents were still yelling after them, but Aubrey was doing what she thought was for the best. They would eventually understand that.

"I stood up for you in there. You need to tell them and soon."

"I know, and I will. Thanks."

Aubrey turned the key and drove off. Life was about to get a hell of a lot more interesting, that was for sure.

~*~

Dropping Ben off had been hard. She knew he needed to go in there alone, but she wanted to help him, protect him. But she couldn't. Ben and Mackenna had to face her parents together, as adults, if they planned on keeping the baby.

How had they been so careless? The minute she found out that Ben was active, she had supplied him with condoms, and gave him the 'don't be an idiot' talk. Apparently, her sex talk skills needed work. Or his listening skills. Probably both.

Aubrey parked her car in the bar parking lot and stepped out. She had been so intent on proving to Henry how not hurt she was when she made the plan of going to the bar, but instead, she just wanted to relax. She didn't care about finding another guy. She didn't care about making anyone jealous. All she wanted to do was have a drink or two and get lost in the music. She needed to let the stress of the day shake off her with every beat of the music.

The place was full as always, and the music was loud. She smiled to herself as she made her way to the bar. The bartender smiled at her and came straight over.

"Well, well, well. Haven't seen you here in a whole week! What have you been up to my lovely, Aubrey?"

"Work. Life. You know, the bullshit that keeps us coming back here to get away from it all. Mind holding my purse behind the bar? I'm solo tonight and don't want to have to hold it while I dance."

"You got it." The bartender took her purse and put it behind the bar then poured her a drink. She downed it in a single shot, tapped the bar top, then went straight to the dance floor, shimmying and shaking to the beat the whole way.

The liquor warmed her from the inside, and the massive amount of bodies on the dance floor warmed her from the outside. After a handful of songs, Aubrey was dying of thirst. Her sweat-slicked skin glistened under the colorful strobe lights illuminating the dance floor. She wiped a few strands of hair that were sticking to her neck and face away as she left the crowd behind to get a bottle of water.

A prickling sensation crawled up her neck, forcing her to look behind her. She knew someone was watching her, and while it wasn't unusual, she also had a feeling she knew exactly who it was.

Henry leaned up against the wall near the dance floor in what Aubrey came to call his Geek Chic look, superhero (she wasn't sure which it was; she was just pretty sure the white circle with a green symbol was some kind of comic book reference) t-shirt and jeans. She gave him the bitch glare and continued on her way to the bar.

She wasn't about to let him ruin her night of stress relief by causing more. Instead of the water she intended to buy, she ordered a double. The bartender smiled as he poured and let her know that the drink was covered.

"Not by that asshole, right?" She asked in a growl, nodding her head in Henry's direction.

"No. That one," he said pointing off to the other end of the bar. The guy that stood there was okay to look at, but even if he had been to die for, she wasn't in the mood. She wasn't rude either, so she raised the glass to him in thanks, and drank her drink.

When she started to feel the buzz come on, she realized that not eating all day, and then drinking and dancing all night wasn't her best choice. She seemed to be making a lot of bad decisions as of late.

"Hey, let me get some water and a burger," she said to the bartender. He nodded his head and punched some numbers into the computer before letting her know her food would be ready in about ten minutes. Aubrey took several small sips of her water, trying to fight back the drunken state she knew was coming, when the man from the end of the bar approached.

"So you like to drink, do you? Bartender said you ordered a double."

"Yeah, sometimes. Thanks for that, by the way."

"No problem. Pretty girl like you shouldn't have to buy her own drinks. Where's the boyfriend?" The man kept moving closer. It wasn't unusual to get advances from men in clubs and bars. Good thing Aubrey knew how to let men down gently.

"Not here tonight, but thanks again." Aubrey stood and went back to the dance floor. Typically, letting a man know she had a 'boyfriend' and walking away did the trick without embarrassing anyone. Not this guy.

"Mind if I dance here?" he asked with a smile, standing next to her.

"Go for it." Aubrey made sure to slowly move away, trying not to be obvious. Apparently, this guy needed obvious. She found him right next to her again, reaching for her waist. "Listen, thanks for the drink and all, but I'm not interested."

"Whatever." Then he left. Sighing in relief, Aubrey returned to the bar where her burger was waiting next to her water bottle.

"Thanks," she said, plopping into the chair and digging in. She picked up the bottle and downed it. Once she was full, she went back to the floor for one last song. Her head was feeling very fuzzy and the room began to spin. She had thought she stopped drinking in time, but apparently not.

Slowly, she lost herself, feeling especially dizzy and the lights were just flashing too bright and too fast. Before she had a chance to fall, two hands wrapped around her waist and held her up. But she didn't want hands on her waist. *Did she?*

Suddenly, she heard loud voices and angry yelling, and she was scooped up into someone's arms. The whole room spun, and she closed her eyes to keep what was in her stomach down, but when the darkness stopped the spinning lights, her body succumbed to the sleep it needed.

Chapter Nine

Aubrey's head pounded and her throat was sore. A repetitive *beep beep beep* echoed into her head. Opening one eye slowly, the light crept in, blinding her. She closed her eye quickly before blinking rapidly, letting her eyes adjust to the bright light infiltrating her room.

Only, it wasn't her room. The walls were white and the bed she laid in was most definitely not hers. Turning from her side, she looked around and realized she was in a hospital room. And Henry sat in a chair beside her bed, snoring softly.

"Hey! Wake up!" she whisper-yelled at him. When he didn't respond, she grabbed the soft paper cup from the bedside table, wadded it into a ball, and threw it at his head. "Wake up!"

He jumped, startled, and then his eyes landed on her. A sense of relief passed over him, his whole body visibly relaxed and a soft smile appeared on his lips. "Oh, thank god you're okay. When the doctors said they had to pump your stomach and you still didn't wake up, I was worried sick."

"What the hell is going on? Why am I in a hospital? What happened?" Aubrey was beginning to freak out. You don't go to the hospital for being drunk. You go home and sleep it off. Unless she drank so much she blacked out. But she didn't remember having more than two drinks.

"You were acting strange all of a sudden on the dance floor. When that guy that had been bugging you all night showed up again, with his arms around you, I knew something wasn't right. I remembered after you sent him packing on the dance floor the first time that he went back to the bar and sat down in your seat until the bartender brought out your food and shooed him away. He had to have put something in your drink. What the hell were you thinking leaving a drink alone in a bar?" His tone had gone from soft to accusatory. She didn't care if he were right. He had no business being angry with her. She wasn't his girlfriend. He wasn't even her friend!

"And how is it any of your business? What I do is none of your concern! Unless it's for my job, you know the one that your company has been stealing clients from left and right that you forgot to tell me you owned!"

"I care about you, Aubrey. And when you act stupid and reckless, I care. Maybe it isn't my business, but oh well. And I am not even getting into business with you right now. You're in a fucking hospital bed because some guy drugged you and tried to take you out of the damn bar. Who do you think stopped him? You know what? Forget it. I thought you had changed since high school, but you are still so self-involved that you can't see beyond what you want and what you think is right, even if it's dangerous."

Henry stood and began pacing the room, his fists balling and releasing, as if he held a stress ball in his hands. Stupid? He thought she was stupid. And she *had* changed. Hadn't she? Her brother was the stupid one. Her eyes widened remembering she needed to get home. She had to be there for Ben when he told their parents about the baby. See, she did think of others.

"Shit, I have to go home. I need to go, now."

"Aubrey, it's four in the morning. Just stay here until a normal hour."

"No. I have to go home. Now." Henry looked at her with irritation but defeat. He knew he wasn't going to win the argument. Even if he kept trying, he couldn't actually stop her from leaving.

"Okay, let me get the nurse." Henry left the room, muttering under his breath. She couldn't hear him, and that was probably a good thing. He saved her from something so horrible that no one should ever have to deal with. She should be grateful. She should have thanked him. But instead she yelled at him. Fuck. She was still a bitch.

When the nurse came in, she had a list of papers about safety and drugs and drinking. She also had the release form which Aubrey signed so quickly that she almost missed the fact that the ginormous bill was paid.

"You paid the bill?" she asked, almost accusatorily. She didn't really have the funds to pay it herself, but she would be damned if she owed him anything.

"Yes, don't argue now. You can yell at me later for helping you out a second time in one night. Whatever you need to get home to is still waiting."

He was right. It wasn't the time, and honestly, she just wanted the whole damn thing to be over. She didn't want to think about what could have happened, and she didn't want to think about owing Henry a ton of money. She just wanted to get to her brother and hoped he didn't think she was bailing on him.

She grabbed her things, and she practically ran through the halls. When she stood before the door to the parking lot, she realized she had no car there. She looked back over her shoulder and saw Henry standing there with a little smile on his face. Bastard knew she couldn't get away from him yet.

"Where's the car?" she asked, giving in to the inevitable.

"Follow me." Henry led the way through the lot to an old beat up black Mustang. She had expected to see the town car, but when he unlocked the door, she knew he wasn't kidding.

"This is yours?" Aubrey took in the dents and scratches in the frame and the patches in the paint. It was not what she expected a billionaire to drive.

"Yup. The first car I ever bought. I love this thing. No amount of money in the world will ever make me get rid of it."

She laughed but climbed in. Henry was full of surprises.

He got behind the wheel and tried to start it up. It took three solid turns of the key before it roared to life.

"She may be old, but she is good to me. Don't make fun," he said with a grin and pulled onto the highway leading out of the city.

"Then you may want to get a tune-up. I don't think it's supposed to be that hard to start a car."

"What do you know about cars?"

"Not much, but I know they should start the first time. I guess I don't need to tell you where to go, do I?"

"I don't know where you live."

"I live at my parent's house."

"Oh, then I do know where to go."

"Go ahead and say it. Say what everyone is thinking. I'm such a child, still living at home."

"Nope, wasn't thinking that."

"Uh, huh. Sure." Aubrey stared out the window and didn't say anything for the rest of the drive. He may not say it, but everyone thinks it. Just another thing he lied to her about. Liars are the reason she won't get involved. She wondered how much of what he had told her was a lie.

Her parent's house came into view just as the sky began turning pink from the rising sun. She opened the door and with a quick, thank you, she climbed out and shut it behind her, ending the conversation. She said thank you. He could take it however he wanted, but it was a giant thank you in her mind. Thank you for the ride, thank you for helping at the bar, thank you for proving that her philosophy of not dating men was the best bet for her to keep her heart intact.

But if that were true, why did it still feel like it was falling apart inside of her with every step she took away from Henry Maximus?

She opened the front door slowly and was glad to see the house was still dark. She crept up the stairs, hoping that Ben was in his room. Her purse and phone hadn't made it to the hospital, so she had no way of knowing if he tried to call.

She slowly opened his bedroom door and saw him asleep in bed. Thankful that he came home, she closed it behind her and went up the second flight of stairs to her room. Her bed was a welcome site. She knew she wouldn't get much time in it before the fireworks between her family started when they all woke, so she dove right in, intending to make the most of the few precious hours she had.

Too bad someone was already in it. Aubrey managed to suppress her scream when Mackenna woke suddenly and jumped back. Aubrey put a hand to her chest and waited for her heartbeat to slow before speaking.

"What are you doing here?"

"I'm sorry! Ben was supposed to wait up and tell you I was here! I'm so, so sorry!" Tears sprang to the young girls eyes, and before Aubrey knew it, Mackenna was sobbing. Something went horribly wrong, and she couldn't be the person to make her night even worse.

"Its okay, it's okay. Just scoot over. I need some sleep."

Mackenna just nodded and moved over. If the girl were surprised by Aubrey wanting to share a bed, she made no mention of it. Aubrey didn't want to have another heart to heart. She wanted sleep. There would be plenty of time for heart to hearts in the morning.

~*~

Daylight spilled into Aubrey's room, pulling her from her deep sleep. She yawned and stretched her arms above her head before looking at the clock. Ten in the morning. How the hell had she slept until ten? Surely, she would have been woken before then?

Sitting up, she looked around the room and found Mackenna sitting in her chair by the bookshelf reading. Why was she still in her room? Where was Ben?

"Morning. Where's Ben?" she asked.

"Still downstairs. Your parents haven't left yet."

Suddenly, it all made sense. Mackenna was hiding out in her room. Aubrey sighed loudly and closed her eyes for a moment. She needed a minute to think. She was all for letting them handle it on their own if that's what they chose, but they had to handle it.

"I'll be right back." Aubrey got up and grabbed a set of clothes from her drawer. She changed in the bathroom quickly (she didn't want her parents to see her in the same clothing as the night before) and went to find her brother.

He was sitting in the living room playing a video game. Their parents were in the house somewhere, but Aubrey didn't see them. She plopped on the couch next to him, making him jump. She could see the worry in his eyes, and he had every right to be worried.

"I tried to call and ask if she could crash in there, but you never answered. You said you were a call away."

"Oh, no, don't turn this around on me. I'm sorry I didn't answer, but that's a whole other conversation that we don't need to get into." She wasn't quite sure she wanted to tell her little brother the situation she had almost found herself in the night before. "You can not hide your girlfriend in my room! What happened?"

Aubrey was whispering just in case her parents were wandering about. She still didn't want to be the one to tell them even though it was becoming apparent she would have to be the one to convince her brother to do so sooner than later.

"They kicked her out. Told her to get rid of it and stop seeing me, or to leave. I thought her dad was going to shoot me."

"I was afraid of that. You have to talk to mom and dad. You can't ignore this. What? Is she going to live up there forever? You never know, Mom and Dad might surprise you. They might be able to help."

"Mom and Dad just think I'm a screw up, and they blame her. You get me. You know I can't turn my back on Mackenna now. Aubrey, I love her but I'm fucking terrified." She could hear the sincerity in his voice and see it in his moist eyes. She knew that look. He was just a step away from shedding a tear, even though he would never admit it.

"I know you do, but that doesn't change anything. She is still pregnant, you still have to tell Mom and

Dad, and you still are going to have to grow up. First things first, go upstairs, get your girl, and talk to Mom and Dad."

The doorbell rang as Ben stood up.

"You get that, I'm going upstairs. Come get me when whoever it is, is gone."

"I will. And then you will talk to them. I can't keep this a secret much longer."

"Yeah, I know."

The bell rang again, and Aubrey called out that she would be right there. As she walked through the house to the front door, she saw a familiar bright green sports car in their driveway. A smile spread across her face, and Aubrey went running, flinging the door open, and launching herself into the arms of the very tall, very handsome, and very gay man who stood on the other side.

"Whoa, there hot stuff. I hope you knew it was me before you mauled me," Greg's deep voice chided in her ear. He was the one friend from college she really missed. He wasn't from her small little town, and while he was only a few years older than she was, it was as if he had lived a lifetime before going to college. She loved hearing his stories about traveling the world and sampling life from different areas.

"Of course, I did. Who else would drive that thing?" Aubrey pulled back from her hug and pointed at the car. It was very unique, that was for sure. The bright green color was only the tip of the iceberg. It had black flame decals, tires that were about two sizes too big for the car (or at least she thought they looked that way), and the entire back window was replaced with plastic slats that could open and close. Aubrey wasn't sure it was legal, but it sure was awesome to look at. "What are you doing here?"

"Just passing through, so I thought I would stop. I hadn't heard anything from you in a while."

Aubrey took Greg inside and told him everything that had been going on in the last week or so. Greg listened and made the appropriate comments when she left an opening for him to do so. It felt good to talk to someone about everything that was going on. By the time she was done, it felt like a fifty ton weight had been lifted from her chest, one stressful worry at a time.

"Seems to me like you have your hands full. Your boss is being an ass, and your boss's boss will give you another chance, Henry... hmm, not really sure what to say there, because I know how you get with men, and your brother, wow, he will figure it out. All you can do is to be there for him. Help him when he needs it, but never give him anything without him having to work for it. He needs to learn some responsibility, and if you fix everything for him, he never will. I hate to leave now, but if I plan on making it to my meeting on time, I need to head out."

"Thanks, Greg. Let me walk you out." Aubrey wasn't sure what he meant about the Henry thing. What did he mean how she gets with men? She is protective of her heart and her time. There was nothing wrong with that. But she also knew he was trying to help, and who knows when she would get to see him again. An argument was the last thing their little goodbye needed.

Aubrey linked her arm through his as they strolled out the front door. Walking him down the steps to his car, Aubrey clung on. Greg was a good friend, and she didn't have many of those around her at the time. It was nice to be able to talk to someone about it.

"Now, when I'm done, I'm going to drive back through here. I want a full report on how you handle Henry. A full report. Got it?"

Aubrey couldn't help but laugh and agree. The two embraced and a soft kiss was exchanged. It wasn't sexual, but simply a show of affection. She had never once thought how it would look to someone else until the moment she pulled away and saw Henry in his car across the street watching—with a jealous gleam in his eye.

Aubrey said goodbye to Greg and watched him pull away before she returned her attention to the man in the car across the street. When she did lock eyes with him, he opened his door and stalked over to her, irritation clearly evident on his face. When he reached her, he handed over her purse. He must have gone back to get it for her.

"Who was that?"

"A friend. And it's your business because?" He had no right to be irritated with her. She did nothing wrong, they weren't a couple, and damn it, she thought her lack of interest was evident (even if it was a big fat fucking lie) with the way she left him that morning. Apparently not.

"Maybe because I fucking care. Apparently, I shouldn't. It seems like you just wanted to get rid of me this morning so damn fast so you could get with that asshole. What was with that fucking car? Does he have money, too? Is that your end game?"

Henry began pacing back and forth. He kept attempting to speak, but stopped himself. The longer she stood there, the more pissed off she was getting. He wasn't helping his case any.

"I have no end game. If you remember, I didn't know who the fuck you were. I didn't ever ask you for money or drinks or to pay my damn hospital bill."

"That's right, Aubrey. You didn't remember me. You were too good for me in high school, and now that you know who I am, you're pushing me away because you're afraid that doesn't work anymore. Heaven forbid your friends find out you hooked up with the biggest geek from high school, right? Well, guess what? I've grown up a bit and I go after what I want. I want you. I wanted you in grade school, I wanted you in middle school, and I wanted you in high school. I was too shy, too quiet, and too afraid to actually say anything. Maybe I'm a glutton for punishment because you sure as hell don't make wanting you easy."

"I never asked you to want me." Aubrey wasn't sure what to say, but getting pissed at her for his feelings wasn't her fault. She could care less about who he was in high school, and she sure as hell didn't like being reminded of who she was at that time, either. She wasn't the one who lied!

"Right, because flaunting yourself in high school wasn't a desperate attempt to make every guy want you? And now? At that bar? The way you move and dance is purely for you, not at all to make guys want you. I think that you need to be wanted, so you can walk away knowing how badly they want you and how much you don't care. You need to still feel in control and popular. You might think you have changed because you have a job that you love, but as a person? It's the same shit wrapped in a different package."

"Fuck you." Aubrey could feel the tears as they formed in her eyes, but she refused to look away from him. If he cared so much, he should see what his words did to her. She may have been distant with him, but she was never hurtful.

"Already did that, remember? So what is this? You know what? Forget that. I have a better idea." Henry started pacing again and mumbling to himself. When he finally turned to her, he had this gleam in his eye as if he had figured out the secret key to a puzzle that had been unsolved for far too long. "I will pay you to not sleep with anyone for the next three months. I think a million dollars is a good price for that. What do you say, you stay celibate for three months, and actually take the time to make real connections with people and you get a million bucks. You give in and fuck someone, you get nothing."

"I'm not a fucking whore, Henry!"

"Whore's get paid to have sex, Aubrey, not abstain from sex. I'm paying you to let go of your old high school bullshit and to grow up, make some real connections with people. When was the last time you can think of that you spent real time with anyone without the end game being sex? And family doesn't count."

Aubrey couldn't answer him. Even when she went out with Bridgette from work, they always ended up splitting ways to hook up with whatever random man for the night. Henry was the only one she could think of, and she wanted to sleep with him, so she went along with the stupid coffee date.

"Exactly. One million dollars for three months. You don't even have to spend them with me if you don't want. But I want you to see how amazing it can be if you let yourself connect. I think you will realize how lonely your life really is right now."

"I'm not lonely. But I'll take your bet anyway. It will be the easiest money I ever make."

Henry smiled at her and shook his head as if he knew something she didn't. Then, he leaned in and kissed her cheek, promptly returning to his car. Aubrey watched as he drove away in his beat up Mustang wondering exactly what she had gotten herself into.

Chapter Ten

Aubrey attempted to put Henry and his ban on sex to the back of her mind. She had more important things to worry about, and they just happened to be hiding out in her bedroom. Aubrey climbed the brick steps back to her front door and ran right into her father.

"Oh, sorry, Daddy. I didn't see you there."

"Apparently. Two men this morning, Aubrey?" Then he let out a big, obviously disappointed, sigh.

"It's not what you think. Greg is a friend, and Henry just stopped by."

"Baby girl, you have got to stop seeing all of these men randomly. You are almost twenty five. Don't you want to meet that special someone? Someone who respects you for you and not for what you are willing to give them? A man like that won't even want to put the time in with someone who doesn't want to do the same."

Aubrey was sick and tired of hearing how because she doesn't like relationships she was somehow a lesser person. Screw that. She didn't need a man in her life. She also didn't need sex. She could get along just fine by herself.

"Dad, please, just don't."

"Fine. I'm just trying to help."

"Of course you are."

Aubrey left her dad standing in front of the door and climbed the stairs to her room. She tried to think of someone, anyone, who she had a real relationship with. The more she thought, the more depressed she got. She had Greg. But did he count when she only saw him once in a blue moon? She never called him to check in, and if they ever got together, it was because he showed up on her doorstep. She didn't even know where he lived. Did she really have a friend, or were they all acquaintances?

The door creaked under Aubrey's hand as she pushed it open. Both her brother and Mackenna jumped at least three feet away from each other. Her bed was disheveled, and so were they.

"Good grief, you two. THIS is what got you into this mess to begin with! And for the love of— NOT MY BED!"

"Would you keep your voice down?" her brother hissed at her. Aubrey narrowed her eyes. She was not the one in the wrong, and she would really like people to start freaking realizing it.

"No. I won't. Have you two figured out what you are going to say to Mom and Dad yet? Any idea of a plan to make this work?"

"Right now, we just need to tell them and let them know that Mackenna will be living here now."

"Let them know? Are you stupid? You need to ask. You can ask if she can stay here but don't be surprised if they say no. What's the backup plan?"

"We don't need one. Mom won't let her grandchild live on the street. She'll agree to Mackenna living here."

"Just remember to keep calm. Don't yell. Don't curse. And don't be an ass. You are the one asking for help. You are the one who screwed up. Not them. You."

Aubrey knew her parents would never agree to that, but they might do what they could to help her with her parents, or help finding her a place to live. But then again, they might surprise her.

"Mackenna, I suggest you keep quiet unless they ask you a question. Then be honest and direct but keep the attitude to a minimum. Our parents have their cool moments, but don't be surprised if they aren't cool enough for this. It's not like the two of you are the pillar of honesty or anything."

"Right. Can we get this over with?" Mackenna asked, her leg bouncing and her pierced lip being gnawed between her teeth. The girl was scared, and rightly so. Aubrey just gave her a soft smile and nodded. She was grateful that she never had to be in Mackenna's shoes. She wasn't even ready for a kid at twenty four, let alone if she had gotten pregnant at fifteen.

The three of them walked down the stairs in silence. Ben and Mackenna went into the living room and sat on the couch holding hands. Aubrey went to collect her parents.

"Mom, Dad? Can you come into the living room? Ben needs to talk to you both."

"Sure, but what is this about?"

"Just promise me you will listen."

"You are scaring me, Aubrey." Her mother stood quickly from the desk chair and moved past her. She must have known it was no use pressing the issue with Aubrey. Her father, on the other hand, was a different story.

"What are we walking into?"

"It's not my place to say anything. It's Ben's."

Her father let out another one of his sighs and stalked past her, following her mother. Taking a deep breath of her own, Aubrey followed them into the living room.

~*~

Aubrey stood in the doorway and watched the horrific scene unfold before her. The minute her parents walked in and saw Mackenna sitting there, so early in the morning, they knew what was going on. They knew what Ben had to tell them.

Before Ben could even confirm their suspicions, their father laid into them. Screaming and yelling about ruining lives and being irresponsible. Their mother just cried. Mackenna sat there, tears flowing from her eyes, but her fists balling up in her lap. Aubrey knew she was pissed at what was being said. But much to her surprise, Ben remained silent. Staring into his lap and waiting for his chance to speak.

Aubrey was quite proud of her little brother for that. At fifteen, she wouldn't have been able to hold her tongue. She was always a handful, doing stupid shit to disappoint her parents. Never a pregnancy, but she had her fair share of hangovers and skipped classes.

When her father had let it all out, he sat beside their mother and just stared at them. Ben looked up from his lap with red rimmed eyes and locked eyes with their father.

"I know we screwed up. I know that we made our future so much harder. I know all of that. I also know that Mackenna doesn't want to have an abortion. I love her, and I will love this baby. Her parents kicked her out when we told them last night. I want her to live here, with us, so she isn't homeless."

He didn't ask like Aubrey told him. She tried to get his attention from behind their parents. She tried to mouth the word ask at him. But he didn't see it. He had listened to everything she told him to do. Up until that point. He could still walk out unscathed if he back peddled and asked. But she knew he wouldn't. She shook her head, and then let it fall against the frame of the door with the rest of her body.

"You want her to live here. Well, I wanted you to have a normal childhood. I wanted you to be an adult before being a parent. I wanted you to meet and marry a good girl, not someone like that! We don't always get what we want, do we?" their father yelled.

"Like what?" Mackenna asked, eyeing the man with a ferocity not usually scene outside of the wild.

"Like a girl who will sleep with a boy at age fifteen. Like a girl who puts holes in her face and colors her hair wild colors and has no self-respect. A girl who has caused nothing but trouble for my son since she met him. Mackenna, I am sure you could be a good girl but right now, you just aren't. If it were up to me, my son would never have gotten involved with you to begin with."

"Apologize to her." Ben demanded. Aubrey stood straight and watched the group carefully. This was going over like a lead balloon, and she couldn't think of a single thing to say to help ease the situation.

"Excuse me?" their father said with a tone laced with poison. Aubrey knew that tone. She had been on the receiving end once or twice before. If Ben were smart, he would stop talking.

"I said, apologize. You can't attack her like that." Ben, apparently, wasn't smart.

"Shut your mouth, Ben," their mother finally said. She had done nothing but cry and watch until then.

"How can you say that? You were a teen mother. I know you were. I saw the pictures in the attic!"

Her mother's eyes widened in shock and looked to their father quickly who looked just as concerned. Aubrey watched the two with real confusion. Her mother wasn't a teen mom. She was married and twenty when Aubrey was born.

"Yes, I was. And I made the right choice to keep my future intact. I let the baby be adopted. That is something you two should consider if you don't want to ruin your chance of a real future."

Aubrey couldn't believe what she was hearing. She had an older sibling out there somewhere. Was it her father's kid or someone else? How old was she when she had the first baby?

"Mom?" Aubrey asked, looking at her mother with real curiosity.

"It's true. Why do you think your father and I are so adamant about you doing things properly? When you don't, situations like these arise. We should have waited until we married. We didn't, and we paid the price. I don't want to talk about this anymore. It was a long time ago. A mistake that I regret, but know I did the right thing in the end. We could have never cared for a child at that age. And neither can you two."

Their mother's attention was back on Ben and Mackenna, who continued to argue with their father. Aubrey's thoughts had left the living room and were somewhere else, wondering who her elder sibling was.

It wasn't until Ben stood with Mackenna's hand in his that she came back to the moment and heard the words that would change everything.

"Get out! I will not have a disrespectful and ungrateful child living in my home! You think you can take care of yourself, your girlfriend, and a child? Then prove it. Pack your shit and get out."

Aubrey watched as her father stormed out of the room, her mother sobbing, and Ben's face contorted into utter despair. Aubrey ran out of the room after their father. He couldn't do that. He had to see reason. Perhaps, if he calmed down, or had someone to talk to about it, he would change his mind.

"Dad! Wait! You can't really want to kick him out. You're just trying to scare them, right?"

"He needs to learn a lesson. When he is ready to apologize, and abide by the rules, he can come back. But I won't let a child talk to me that way, and I certainly won't let his girlfriend, pregnant or not, live with him like a little married couple. I am going to call her parents today, try and smooth things over, or at least get an open conversation going, but no. He has to leave. At least for a few days."

Aubrey could understand his position, and was glad he was going to help even if he didn't tell Ben and Mackenna that, but she had no idea where they would go in the mean time.

"I get that, but Dad, he has been terrified of telling you for two days, and you just confirmed his fears. You should at least tell them you will speak to Mackenna's parents."

"You've known? Why didn't you tell us?"

"Right, because telling you and causing not only a fight between you and Ben, but between him and I, was the best thing to do. I didn't let him ignore it. He told you, didn't he? I found out yesterday. He told you today. I would say that's not horrible. And now that you kicked him out, he needs someone in this family to be able to talk to."

"No. You will not speak to him either. He needs to learn, and we have to do that as a family unit. When he is ready to apologize, he may come home and do so. Until then, we are a united front, once he steps out that door, that's it."

"And if he doesn't apologize? What then? You will just pretend you have no son or a grandchild on the way?"

"He will. It may take him a bit, probably until his friends parents catch wind of why he is spending the night so often, but he will come back, and we can deal with the whole situation."

"Right." Aubrey shook her head and walked away from her father. If he thought that was going to work, he was crazy. Ben wasn't going to apologize for standing up for Mackenna. Her father would never have allowed anyone to speak about their mother that way, and he sure as hell wouldn't apologize for anything that came out of his reaction to it. Ben and their father were much more alike than either was willing to admit.

"I mean it, Aubrey," he called after her. She knew he did. She also knew she would never let her brother be homeless. It was time to get an apartment.

The next week went by in a blur. Aubrey did nothing but work, drive to and from work, or scour the papers and internet for a place to live. Ben and Mackenna had been house hopping their friend's places, but it was getting old for everyone involved.

Lying on her bed, Aubrey circled two more apartments to check out on her lunch break that day. If it worked out, she would have to find out about school transfers and technical guardianship for Ben, unless she could convince her mother to sign the papers and help—without telling her father.

When her alarm went off, not that she had been sleeping, and she got up and dressed for the day. With the paper tucked under her arm, she headed downstairs and out the door without a word to her parents. Ever since her intentions became clear, she was on the do not talk to list as well as her brother. She really hoped they would come around.

Rain poured down on her car as her windshield wipers tried valiantly, yet unsuccessfully, to clear her view. Aubrey pulled off to the side of the road and fished her phone out of her purse. If the weather kept up this badly, it would take her forever to make it to the office.

The phone rang, but even the sound of the ring was static-y. Aubrey watched the clouds darken before her eyes and a flash of lightening lit the sky. A second later, thunder boomed.

"Viola Gaming Industries, how may I direct your call?" the receptionist answered.

"Fiona, its Aubrey. Can you put me through to Mike?"

"Sure, but beware, he is in a mood." The phone line clicked over to the hold music, which just so happened to be game soundtracks. Aubrey racked her brain trying to figure out why Mike was in such a mood.

"What is it, Aubrey?" Mike's gruff voice said into the phone.

"Just that I'm stuck on the side of the road with this damn storm, and I might be late if it doesn't lighten up here soon."

"What? Oh, right, the storm. Be careful and get here when you can." The line went dead. Aubrey checked to see if she lost signal, but no, she hadn't. Mike had hung up on her. Aubrey stared at her phone a moment longer before slipping it back into her purse. Shutting the car off, she watched the storm over her.

A loud knock came from the window beside her, causing her to practically jump three feet. With a hand to her chest and the other on the window button, she let it down just an inch to see who stood there.

A very wet Henry stood there, worry evident in his eyes. The coat he wore looked to be more of a hooded zip up sweater (with a Batman logo across the chest) than a rain jacket. He was soaked to the bone. Another flash of lightening streaked across the sky, causing a beautiful reflection to dance in his eyes.

"What the hell are you doing out there?" she demanded.

"I saw your car on the side of the road, inches from a large ditch, in the middle of a damn thunderstorm. I was seeing if you were okay."

His concern was touching, even though she wished she could be annoyed. "Well, I'm fine, as you can see. I just couldn't see through the rain."

"Okay. I guess I'll be on my way then?" Henry looked back at his Mustang, then back to her and waited for her response. Did she want to be alone for who knows how long in the middle of a storm?

"Or you could wait with me?"

The smile that stretched across Henry's face was the only answer she needed. When he disappeared from her side, she quickly rolled the window up and pressed the unlock button just before Henry reached the passenger side. The wind howled when he opened the door, and nearly took her door clean off her car with its strength before Henry was able to close it.

Once the two were in the confined space together, Aubrey started to think twice about her decision.

"So," he said.

"So," she repeated.

"How's your week been?"

"Long. Yours?"

"Same, but I know what happened in mine. I am much more interested in yours. Want to talk about it"

Did she? No. But if she didn't, he might consider that not opening up, not allowing herself to make connections not based on sex. She wouldn't lose the bet on a technicality. Not that she actually wanted to take his million dollars. Too close to charity, but she wanted to win the bet anyway. She wanted to shove his money in his face. Aubrey Vincent couldn't be bought.

"Well, it started with a trip to a hospital, then being practically called a slut by not only a guy I slept with recently but also my father. I was offered a ton of money to change my ways and turn into a better person, then my brother knocks up his girlfriend, our father kicks him out, tells me I can't talk to him if I live there. I've been apartment hunting to help my brother, and now I am stuck in the middle of a storm, in my car on the side of the road, with a man who does nothing but infuriate me while being so damn sexy I can't help but want to fuck the shit out of him, but I can't because he imposed a no sex rule. How's that?"

"Sounds like a hell of a week. So, apartments, huh? What have you looked at so far?" Henry looked at her, cool as a damn cucumber, completely glossing over the sex thing. She was shocked, but also a little expecting it somehow.

"I looked at a place on 7th, but it was small and dirty. Then a place on Elm, which was okay, but the rent was insane. And another on Forrest Ave, but the whole area gave me the heebie-jeebies. I had planned on checking out this new apartment building that just opened last month later today, but I don't think that's going to happen."

"The apartments on Kendall? Those are really nice."

"Thanks, I will. I just hope they are not only affordable, but a decent place. I mean, if all goes according to plan, my brother, and his girlfriend, and their soon to be baby will be there. I don't want a baby in crack alley, ya know?"

Henry just laughed and repeated 'crack alley' then shook his head. "You never cease to amaze me, Aubrey."

"Um, thank you?"

"Relax, it was a compliment. I wish you could see yourself the way most of the rest of the world does. I see you, the real you. I may not know you all that well yet, but I see you. I always have."

The conversation was beginning to turn uncomfortable for Aubrey. It felt like she was under a microscope with a sexy scientist staring down at her, flaws and all.

"So, uh, what about you? How was your week?" She wasn't really sure she wanted to hear how he saw her, or what the hell he was thinking with that stupid bet, but if it got the focus off her, it would be worth it.

Aubrey wouldn't look Henry in the eyes, so she found a loose string on her shirt, or a bit of dirt under her fingernail to occupy her attention.

"Well, I was going crazy. There's this girl that has been on my mind for so long, and I knew that when I reconnected with her, I should be honest. But she had no idea who I was. She didn't remember me. I thought that maybe that was in my favor. She wouldn't think of me as the geeky kid no one liked in high school. She could see me for who I am now. But then, she didn't know who that was either. And it was so refreshing. She wanted to spend time with Henry. Not Henry the billionaire. And lord, was she sexy. But she kept me at arm's length. But eventually, we both gave in and had the most mind blowing night in the back of my town car.

"I wish it had never happened though. The minute it did, she was done with me. Or trying to be. I also wish I had told her who I was when I found out she worked for the company hell bent on blaming me for their short comings. I just couldn't figure out how without coming off like an asshole."

Henry was staring at her. She couldn't see him. She was, after all, doing everything she could to avoid his eyes, but she could feel him. He was waiting for a reaction out of her. Anyone would be after saying all of that. But what could she say? No, she wouldn't have cared who he was? She didn't want to believe it would have mattered, but it might have, and that thought scared her. She was an awful person.

"So then in my attempt not to be an asshole, I was a bigger one, showing up at a meeting I knew she would be at but she had no idea I would, just to see her again and to tell her the truth. And then she wouldn't listen, not that I blamed her. When I saw this girl at the bar, being taken advantage of, I saw red. I was angrier than I ever had been in my life and did something stupid that I will never regret. I beat the shit out of the guy and got my girl to the hospital. The next morning, when I went to check on her, she was with another man. I watched this girl that I had realized I had fallen for kiss another man, and I said some stupid shit, but I still stand by it. I did it wrong, but a promise is a promise, and the idea that I will have three months to win her over gives me hope. Oh, and when I got back to the city, I got arrested for the first time in my life, was given a fine, and I now have a record. All because the asshole who drugged a girl couldn't handle being beat up by a geek."

Aubrey turned to face Henry so quickly that she nearly pulled a muscle in her neck. He was arrested because of her? And there she was being an ungrateful bitch. Her hand reached out to his before she knew what she was doing and squeezed. She didn't know what to say, but she wanted him to know she did hear him.

A small smile touched his lips, warming her heart, and then his other hand came to rest on top of hers, cocooning her beneath his warmth.

"I didn't know."

"I know," he said.

"That asshole pressed charges?" she asked a little awkwardly. It was her fault, after all. She felt horrible.

"Yeah, but once I told the judge why I did what I did, she went easy on me."

"I wish I could prove he did it. Then I could return the favor. The hospital should have my tox screen, right?"

"Do you really want to go through with that?"

"I know I should. I mean, if he had the stuff to put in my drink, he could do it again."

"I'll ask the owner if where you were sitting is covered by the cameras. I know the dance floor is covered. They got every single second of me pounding into him."

"Thank you." She found herself thanking him again for one thing but meaning so much more. She knew that, at some point, she would have to admit that Henry meant more to her than she would like. She just didn't know if that point were then.

"It's not a big deal. Anyone with half a heart would have done the same if they knew what I did."

"It is a big deal, and no, they wouldn't have. You did though."

"Aubrey," he said, and then trailed off. She looked at him, this man who was funny and caring, and kind, and generous, and smart, and… lucky for her, oh-so-gorgeous. She couldn't comprehend what he saw in her. She was shallow, and apparently, slept around and still lived in her parents fucking attic. She couldn't keep a relationship going, either platonic or romantic. She was a mess, and he was perfect, even if he did have a thing for superheroes.

Aubrey leaned in and brushed her lips lightly against his, before pulling back just enough to look in his eyes, but still close enough to let his warm breath wash over her skin.

"What are you doing?" he whispered, his eyes searching hers,

"I don't know." She leaned in again, less hesitant than before, and pressed her lips firmly against his.

His hands moved from where she held them and ran up her arms to her shoulders and pressed slightly, breaking their kiss.

"This isn't what I wanted, Aubrey."

His words were as if a knife had wound itself into her stomach. "Then what did you want?"

"I want to know you. I want to know you in a way that no one else does. And I want you to know me, really know me. Not because I want you to, but because you want to, because not knowing me causes you so much heartache that the thought of walking away from me is torture in itself. I want you to think of me and feel for me what I do for you."

Aubrey looked away. She didn't want him to see the tears escaping from her eyes. She didn't know if she could ever give him what he wanted. And what she could give him he didn't want. The rain had stopped at some point without either of them noticing.

"Rain's done," she said, letting him know the conversation, and the moment they had found themselves in, were done, too.

"So it is. I guess I will be on my way then. I'll see you around, Aubrey." Henry opened the door and left her sitting there. It was exactly what she wanted to happen, but for whatever reason she hated to see him go.

"I do think of you," she whispered to no one. A stray tear fell from her eye before she wiped it away. The car rumbled to life, and she pulled back onto the road. She dared not look in her rear view, because if she saw him, she just might turn around and give him everything he wanted. It would be good for a while, possibly great, but something would happen, and it would all come crumbling down around them, leaving them both broken and hurting. Was it really worth it?

~*~

Aubrey made it to the apartments on Kendall after all. And Henry was right. They were perfect. She signed the lease right then and there. Within two days, she had moved in.

Getting her mother to agree to transfer Ben's school wasn't quite so easy, but she had done it. No one wants to see their child on the street, even if they were trying to teach them a life lesson. At fifteen, that is too harsh of a lesson.

Ben and Mackenna had their own room and Aubrey had hers—on the other side of the apartment. There were also rules that she came up with, and that was the hard part. She tried to think of things that were fair and more like a roommate than a mother.

Aubrey called them into the bare living room, and they all sat on the floor in a circle. She had enough money to get the apartment, just not furnish it. She would in time, and it would be perfect. She just knew it.

"Okay, I know that we said I didn't want to be mom, but I think we need some rules. All of us. So let me say what I have to first, and then we can discuss anything you want. Got it?"

Her brother and his girlfriend just nodded their heads, their hands clasped together between them on the floor.

"First off, you will both get a job for after school and weekends. Mackenna, when you are too far along to work and right after the baby, of course that doesn't apply. Second, you will help with bills, and you will put money away to pay for that baby. Neither of you has any real idea how much this kid is going to need. You will need to have money for all of that, too. Third, you will stay in school. Period. No ifs, ands, or buts about it. You will be in the apartment by midnight. My room is mine, your room is yours, but the rest of the apartment is for all of us, so the cleaning of it will be on all of us. Any questions?"

She thought she did a good job with the rules. The only one she thought stepped out of roommate boundaries was the curfew, but they were fifteen, after all, and she would be worried sick if they didn't come home.

"How are we supposed to get jobs?" Mackenna asked with an attitude. Aubrey looked at her with a tilted head and raised eyebrows. Mackenna didn't back down though. "I mean it, look at us. We are just two kids, and I'm pregnant. No one is hiring, and they really won't hire me knowing I will be leaving in eight months. And Ben hasn't ever worked before. You have to have experience to work. You said you got the second bedroom to help us. Not trick us into paying your bills."

"Whoa, whoa, whoa, little girl. I am helping you. Do you think that you can do nothing and take care of a baby? How do you know no one is hiring? Have you looked for a job? How do you think people get experience to begin with? They get crappy first jobs that pay little, but at least put some money in their pocket. You will not live here for free. I am not your mother. I will not pay for you. Ben, I suggest you check your girlfriend before I kindly tell her this was a bad idea and to get out."

Aubrey stood and left the living room. She had never heard Mackenna talk like that before. Where was the girl that was always so respectful to her, the sweet girl who cried on her shoulder?

Her room was a disaster of boxes. The bedrooms were the only rooms that actually had anything in them, and boy was hers stuffed full. The attic in her parents' house was much larger than the bedroom in the apartment. But it was hers. She had even given Ben and Mackenna the master bedroom because they would need the extra room for a crib and having access to a bathroom in the middle of the night would help when it came to pregnancy stuff. At least, that's what she had heard.

A soft knock came from behind her and when she turned, Ben was standing there. She didn't say anything to him, and she just waited for him to speak. She knew if she waited, and stared at him, long enough he would break.

And he did.

"Please don't kick her out. She just isn't used to rules like those. You know, ones that were more than just be a good girl and do what I say ones. Her parents never made her work for anything, no chores, no nothing. They just bought what she wanted. I'll talk to her and right after school tomorrow I will make sure we both go and get applications. I promise."

"I know, but she needs to grow up now. She isn't in their house anymore, and pretty soon she will be the one buying a kid stuff. And remember, for a first job, you can't be a job snob. Nothing is beneath you if they are willing to pay you to do it. Scratch that. Nothing legal is beneath you. Flip burgers, clean toilets, whatever. Just do it, do it well, and work hard. You will be fine. It's not going to be easy, but I know you can do it, Ben."

Her little brother stepped into her room and wrapped his giant arms around her in a hug.

"Thanks," he said then left her room.

Aubrey closed the door behind him and fell back on her bed. *In her apartment.* She just hoped that she could manage not to screw it up. She had more than herself to worry about, and her failure would mean her brother and her future niece or nephew would be on the street and that was not okay. She couldn't fail this time. She wouldn't.

Chapter Eleven

The line at the coffee shop near her apartment was long. So long that when she left that morning she was going to be early, but her craving for caffeine was going to make her late.

Living just six blocks from her office, she decided to save on gas and the environment and walk to work. But walking led her by the amazing aroma of roasting coffee and baking goodies. Her nose gave her no choice but to investigate. Unfortunately for her, the rest of the damn noses in the city must have done the same thing. She should have driven.

By the time she walked out with her steaming cup, she had exactly two minutes to walk the five blocks that remained. Aubrey walked as quickly as she could while carrying her shoulder bag and holding her coffee. When the crosswalk at the busiest intersection in the area turned red just before she got to it, she knew that she was in no way making it in on time.

With as much time as she had taken off to find the apartment and move in that week, she knew she was on thin ice. Just as she was checking her watch to see exactly how late she was going to be, a stranger bumped right into her, causing hot coffee to spill down the front of her light pink blouse, both scalding her and ruining her clothing.

"Fuck!" she yelled, dropping her bag to pull her shirt away from her skin. Aubrey turned, venom in her eyes, ready to pounce on whoever it was.

"Chill lady, it's just a shirt," the stupid kid said.

"Just a shirt? What about the skin that has been burnt off under it?" she seethed. Just before she could go off on a rather curse-filled tirade, a black town car stopped beside the road. The window rolled down and Henry looked out at them.

"Need a ride?" he asked, looking back and forth between her and the stranger who was two seconds away from having his head bit off.

"Yeah," she said, never taking her icy glare off the man in front of her. "Fuck you," she said then opened the car door and slid in beside Henry.

"Are you okay?"

"I don't know. It burns like a bitch. I just got that damn coffee, too. I didn't even get to taste it. I guess that's what I get for waiting in line for twenty minutes to spend five bucks on a coffee when I make just enough to get by."

"Buying yourself something nice once in a while isn't going to kill your budget. Let me see." Henry reached forward toward her shirt, taking her completely off guard.

"What are you doing?" she asked backing up quickly.

"I wanted to see your stomach, see how bad the burn is."

"Oh, right." Aubrey lifted her shirt just enough to show the red welts that were covering her stomach. The searing pain went all the way to her bra line. Thank god she wore a formed cup bra. That kind of burn would be hell on nipples. "Mind if we go to my place before you take me to work? I need to get a different shirt."

"Do you have burn cream? This looks pretty bad," he said, ghosting his fingers over one welt. Aubrey winced and jerked away. "Sorry! Oh, I didn't mean to hurt you."

"I don't have any kind of first aid stuff at the apartment. We just moved in and all. The only rooms that have much are the bedrooms. Ben and I are going shopping this weekend to get other stuff we might need."

"Okay, then first we stop at the pharmacy, then I take you home, then to work."

"Won't that make you late?" The amount of care he was putting into helping her was sweet. And she did need the cream.

"That's the good part about being the boss, I'm allowed." The grin he gave her set her heart on fire, beating a million times a minute, causing her to smile right back.

Henry pushed the little intercom button to tell the driver where to go, and Aubrey watched him with affection. He definitely was someone special. If only she could make sure she was good enough for him.

~*~

By the time Aubrey had gone to the pharmacy, gotten home, changed, and gotten back to work, she was more than a half hour late. There was a note at the front desk asking her to go straight to Mike's office.

Dread sat heavy in her stomach. This was it. She signed a year lease, and she was about to lose her job. At least, if she could keep herself from pouncing on Henry's dick for three months, she could collect a cool million. She had no interest in anyone else's appendages, which scared her like crazy. She laughed to herself as she entered the elevator. Who had ever heard of such a crazy challenge? Not having sex was the easy part.

As long as she stayed away from anywhere private with Henry.

The office had its usual busy atmosphere about it with assistants running around, phones ringing, copiers working. But something felt different. Perhaps it was her impending unemployed status.

Aubrey looked over to her desk by Jenna's office to see the temp packing her things in tears. Jenna looked up at just the right moment and locked eyes with her through the glass wall and glared. She didn't know what she had done to get on Jenna's bad side, but she didn't like it.

Mike's door was shut and Bridgette was nowhere to be seen, so she walked up and knocked on his door. Mike opened it quickly with a quizzical look. If Bridgette were anything like her, she would never let anyone knock if it could be helped. She would always buzz Jenna to tell her about a guest. Mike got no buzz.

"Aubrey, I expected you a while ago."

"Sorry, there was a coffee incident that left me with a pretty nasty stain on my shirt and matching one on my stomach. I had to take care of that, but I came in as fast as I could. What did you need to see me about?"

Mike looked around at the people behind her then opened his door further. "In here."

"Okay?" she said as more of a question than a statement. Aubrey walked into his office. Mike usually kept his space as clean as a whistle. Not a paper out of place, not a pen lying randomly on the desk. But right then, it looked like a tornado had hit it. "What the hell happened in here?"

"I've been pouring over contract after contract. Apparently, when Buffet, Hodges, and Keith signed with us ten years ago, there was a clause in there. They can take their games and their business elsewhere after eight years. Somehow, the other companies found out and are all trying to steal them away. I've been making sure the other contracts don't have the same clause. I wish Peterson still worked here, so I could slap him silly for putting it in there!"

The enormity of what was going on wasn't lost on her. Those three clients alone made up fifty percent of their business. They produced at least thirty games a year each. And they all sold and sold well. If Viola lost them, it was only a matter of time before Viola itself was lost.

"What can I do?" Aubrey looked around, itching to start cleaning up for him. She knew that the disarray of his office was adding to his stress level, even if he didn't realize it. She wasn't a neat freak, but it was starting to bug her, too.

"I need you to take this file," Mike thrust a large manila envelope at least two inches thick at her, "and go through it. Find a new way to market the old games. I think that is going to be our saving grace. While every other company is going to focus on the present and the future, we are going to promise them the same devotion to new games they have always gotten, but we want to start a back log campaign, too. I just need to find a way to make ten year old games interesting again. You come up with out-of-the-box stuff. I need you to do that for me now. Can you?"

"On games that work on consoles that are outdated and not sold anymore?"

"I know, sounds crazy, but just try to come up with something."

"I will do my best. I promise."

"I don't think I need to tell you how badly we need to keep these contracts, do I?"

"No, you don't. I'll get started right away. I'll be upstairs if you need me."

Mike nodded his head and went back to the pile of papers on the little table in front of his couch. Aubrey left Mike's office and headed straight for the elevator. Upstairs was a dusty old office that no one used any longer. It had become her quiet area, and only Mike and Jenna knew about it. No one would bother her, and she could concentrate completely. It helped her get in the zone.

After three hours, she had nothing. And she was starving. Aubrey grabbed her purse, the file, and headed out for lunch. Perhaps food would help her think better.

The sandwich shop down the street was usually pretty quiet. She was able to order her turkey and Swiss on rye and take over the table in the back corner with ease.

A bell jingled, and a commotion broke Aubrey's attention away from her work. Henry had come in followed by a horde of young boys holding game cases in their hands, waving them at Henry. They were begging for autographs.

Aubrey couldn't help but laugh. Henry had groupies. Just not the ones most men would want. But Henry wasn't most men, and he smiled and signed, and then asked the kids if he could eat his lunch in peace. They all left with big smiles of their own and hugging their new treasures tightly to their chest.

Henry slumped into the chair about halfway from the front of the shop and sort of hid behind a potted plant. She watched as he took a breath or two then studied the menu that she had memorized. When he stood to order, she listened carefully. She felt that a person could learn a lot from what another ordered, and how they ordered, when they weren't trying to impress anyone.

To her surprise, he ordered a turkey and Swiss on rye. But he said hold the mustard. She shook her head in disappointment. Mustard was key to the sandwich. What was he thinking?

"You ordered it wrong," she said loudly, making him jump and spin in her direction. The stress from his face melted away and was replaced by a smile.

"Oh, I did, did I? And what did I do wrong?"

"Turkey and Swiss on rye *has* to have mustard. It's just the way it was meant to be. Like PB&J or bologna and cheese. Anything else is just wrong."

"What if I don't like mustard?"

"Then I'd say you've never had it on turkey and Swiss on rye. I don't like mustard on anything else, either, but on this sandwich? It's a must."

"Is that so?"

"Yup."

"Excuse me, Could you add mustard to that, after all?" Henry said to the man behind the counter making his sandwich. Then he turned back to Aubrey. "Happy?"

"Yes, and so will you when you taste it."

"And if I don't like it?"

"Then I'll buy you another one without the mustard."

"Deal."

Henry took his sandwich from the counter guy and came to sit at the table with her. Aubrey quickly put her work away, not sure how she should handle the competing company thing between them. Henry watched her but said nothing. Once the table was clear, he opened the wrap around his sandwich and eyed it, almost as if it might turn into a monster and eat him instead.

"Just try it. It's not going to kill you." Aubrey took a bite of her own sandwich to prove her point.

"Here goes," Henry said before picking his sandwich up and taking a great big bite out of it. Aubrey watched as his contorted face slowly relaxed as he chewed and swallowed. He sat his sandwich back down and stared at her. For three whole minutes. Aubrey counted each agonizing second. Finally, he spoke. "Okay, maybe mustard does belong on this."

"YES!" she cheered, punching the air. Henry laughed and took another bite.

"So is this where you come for lunch every day?" he asked as soon as his mouth was empty. Hot and manners—she was doomed.

"Not every day. Planning on stalking me?"

"I wouldn't call it stalking, just looking for good places to eat. I haven't lived around here since the end of senior year."

"No? Where have you been?"

"Up until a little bit ago, I lived in New York. Seemed like a good time to come back for good. I had to check in on the branch here in the city and see the parents, and I kind of found what I've been missing in New York. It never really felt like home. So many people but not one you could honestly say who the hell they were. I mean, the way we grew up? Mrs. Janner down the street knew everyone, and knew exactly what they were up to. Annoying at times, sure. But at least you knew you were never really alone."

The weight of his words hit Aubrey. It was true, and it was one of the reasons she wanted out. The city kept her anonymous. She didn't have to worry about the looks she got when she went out and about. Poor Aubrey couldn't cut it at college. Poor Aubrey can't keep a man. Or what was worse, when she heard them pitying her parents for having such a screw-up as a kid. And there was Henry, longing to go back.

"Must be nice to not have anything to run from. I'm sure everyone is so proud of you. I've got the opposite."

"Actually, it's not like that at all. I wasn't a favorite, remember? I was the geeky kid with the parents who cleaned the school at night. They knew who I was, but no one really cared much about what we did. Now they try to act as if they've always been there. But, the few who really did care back then? They are worth it. My parents. You."

"Me?" she asked, completely taken off guard. She knew he was interested, and that they had a connection, but to move on the off chance that she may come around seemed a bit extreme. She knew first hand that moving for someone else was just dumb.

"Yes, Aubrey, you. I don't know why that surprises you. I've told you that I want you. How can I ever expect this to work if I'm living someplace so far we have to take a plane to see each other? If this never happens, I can always go back if I want to. I didn't sell the apartment."

What could she say to that? She didn't want to encourage him, but at the same time, as much as she tried to fight it, she didn't want to send him away either. Not that he would go. He's proven that a time or two.

"Well, it was really nice having lunch, but I have to get back to the office. I have a lot of work to do."

"Did you get the promotion even after what happened with Mrs. Stine? I really didn't want to mess your chances up, and I realized after the fact that talking to you right after presenting was probably a stupid move."

"I don't know yet, but it's probably best if we don't talk about work. Rival companies and all. I'll see you around I'm sure. Bye, Henry." Aubrey picked her things up and walked out the door. She could feel his eyes on her all the way out the door and down the street until she turned at the first street. It wasn't the way to the office, but she knew if she looked back over her shoulder, Henry's eyes would be fixed on her.

Aubrey walked back to her building, thoughts of moving boxes and Henry dancing around in her head. He really believed in them. He believed she could let him in and that she would fall for him. Falling was the easy part, letting him in and opening up to yet another mistake, another heartbreak, wasn't so easy.

Why couldn't he be like other men she knew who were perfectly content to have fun one night, and then be on their way the next morning? Wasn't no strings attached sex a man's dream? Apparently, not Henry's.

When Aubrey walked back into the office, she was done thinking about Henry. She would be focused and smart, and she would think of the best damn way to market the old games for the old systems that most kids no longer even knew what they were. She could do it. She just had to think. Really, really damn hard.

As she walked through the office on her way to let Mike know she was back from lunch, she saw Jenna waiting by her old desk. Her arms were crossed, and her eyes narrowed, looking directly at Aubrey. Apparently, she was waiting for her and not just standing around for the fun of it. Go figure.

"Okay, what did I do this time?" she asked, exasperated. Placing her bag and her work on her old desk, she just waited for Jenna to speak. She didn't understand where this person had come from. Jenna used to be so cool and treated her almost friendly. She wanted *that* Jenna back.

"Where have you been? Mike told me the job he gave you. That could very well make or break this company. Not all of us are lucky enough to live at home without any bills. This isn't a time to be messing around!"

"Whoa. I have my own apartment for one, and for two, I was at lunch, and I worked through half of it. I know this is important. I'm not stupid."

"Not stupid, just falling for Henry Maximus's charming ways of getting all the intel on this company to build his and ruin ours."

"You don't even know Henry. Or is that the problem? Did he turn you down?" Aubrey knew she was crossing a line, and as soon as it was out of her mouth, she regretted it. One word from Jenna to Mike, and she could be out of a job completely.

"Oh, no, honey. I had him over two years ago. But I was trying to find out secrets of his company and kept tight lipped about ours. Shame he wouldn't give anything up. He is quite talented in bed, isn't he?"

The news was like a knife to the gut, ten times over. Aubrey could feel the tears threatening to fall, and for no real reason. It was a long time ago, and she couldn't even claim Henry as her own. Of course, he had been with other women. But to have one standing right in front of her sucked.

"Your point is? Well, besides being a cradle robber anyway. Two years ago, Henry was twenty three. That's what? A twenty year age gap?"

"He was begging for it," she said with a smirk and tilt of her head. "My point is, don't get any ideas. You were my personal assistant, and if you don't keep your head away from the competition and on those stupid old games, you might as well reacquaint yourself with the coffee machine."

"Why don't you just let me do my work? I don't know what I did to make you act this way toward me, but I never did anything intentionally." Even though she was pissed, she wished she could reverse whatever the hell had happened, and make them the great team they were before. Not that she wanted to go back to being a personal assistant. She wanted that market research position. Especially now that she had rent to pay and a brother and soon to be niece or nephew to make sure had a home.

"Good luck. Mike basically gave you the job no one wanted. It's impossible, and it will never work."

"Then I guess we are all screwed."

Aubrey didn't let Jenna reply. She just picked her things back up and headed for her quiet place. Aubrey spent the next four hours pouring over old data. The problem was—it was old. The games were old and out dated. Sure, adults would feel some nostalgia for the games of their childhood, but those that still played were not the majority. A marketing plan for them wouldn't be enough to keep the clients at Viola. Aubrey opened her laptop and logged onto one of the most popular gaming forum sites online. With over a million registered users, plus a daily guest count of thirty five thousand, it was a good place to get feedback anonymously.

First, she started a thread asking if users had ever played a handful of the games she was supposed to figure out a plan for. Then she did another post under a thread for 'cool game ideas' where she gave a brief summary of a couple others. Then she waited.

As she expected with the first post, she got a lot of 'when I was a kid' type of responses. But what she hadn't expected was the second thread exploding with excitement. She had comments ranging from how amazing the games sounded to asking if anyone knew of any games similar. When the older gamers started commenting on how it sounded like the originals from twenty years prior, she had her idea. It was a long shot, and it would take a lot of funding, but it could work.

Proud of her work for the day, and eager to get home to relax with a glass of wine, pajamas, and a marathon of mindless television for a night, she packed up. No one could sour her mood. She had a solid idea, and when she went to work the following day, she would make a plan of action that would include the costs and the target market, and she would blow their socks off.

The office was practically empty as she left the building. When she realized it was yet again almost seven at night, she knew why. The front door swung open, allowing the cool night air breeze to chill her bare arms. She hadn't worn a jacket that morning and she was wishing she had. While the office was a short walk, it was going to be a chilly one.

Aubrey rubbed her hands up and down her goose bump covered arms, but the smile never left her face. She was finally doing something right. She had a place of her own (even if her brother was living with her), she had a job that was going places (even if the company was on the brink), and she was happy (even if she wasn't having sex). It was a lot of 'even ifs' but it didn't matter. What mattered was that she was in a better place than she was just a month before.

Aubrey decided to take a detour on the way home, throwing the idea of wine and television out the window. It was a dancing kind of night. She wanted to feel the beat of the music flowing through her and get lost in it. She wanted to let loose.

The bar came into view, and the music floated on the air all the way down to her three blocks away. Aubrey walked past the long line of people waiting to get in and stopped right next to Kevin, the head bouncer who was built like a house. Looking up into his eyes, she grinned and batted her lashes. She and Kevin went way back. He would let her in. There was never a doubt.

"All right, go on." She leaned up and kissed his cheek as she passed by, and then jumped in surprise at the pat on the ass she received. "What? It was there."

"Thanks, Kevin!" Aubrey just ran inside. She should have expected it, but she never did. Kevin went to college with her—before she was kicked out—and was in the fraternity that was opposite her sorority. They partied together many times, with and without clothes. But now he was just an old friend who let her into the bar before everyone else. They hadn't been together like that in many years.

The dance floor was a sea of bodies moving together like waves in an angry storm. Limbs moved and shook to the fast beat that flowed through the building. Aubrey looked to the bar to see it was just as packed.

The energy in the room was just what she needed. She loved being in a thrash of people and noise. She could get out of her own head and just be. Aubrey pushed her way to the bar and flagged the bartender over.

Suddenly, all she could think about was the last time. She didn't remember much, but she wasn't so sure a drink was a good idea. She wasn't with anyone to look out for her. Surprisingly, Henry was nowhere to be seen. While she had never wanted him to show up, she began to expect it, and knowing he was there made her feel something—safe maybe, or just more comfortable. Either way, she didn't feel that way then. She felt on edge, and actually, rather lonely.

Out of habit, she took at the group around her. She could hang out with a guy for the night and dance before heading home. She could enjoy her night without the release that sex brought. She loved the high she got when she felt wanted and sexy and actually got to orgasm. But she wouldn't. She couldn't. Unless of course, she could keep it a secret.

How would Henry actually know what she did or didn't do?

When the bartender got to her, he smiled and said hi. She ordered a bottle of water and made sure to replace the cap after each drink. The man who sat at the end of the bar had been watching her, smiling at her. He was tall and dark skinned, and very well built. She could dance with him and enjoy his presence then head home for her wine and television.

Just a few dances wouldn't hurt a thing. Aubrey swayed her hips ever so subtly as she walked over to Dark and Yummy. That was what she dubbed him for the night.

"Want to dance?" she asked with a small smile. His eyes started at her feet and worked their way up her body, lingering in all the places that used to make her feel wanted, but actually made her feel a little awkward.

"Absolutely." Dark and Yummy stood and was a good foot taller than she was. He gripped her hand, a little tighter than Henry would, and pulled her to the dance floor. As he moved his hips and hands to the beat and along her body, she knew he could dance. She used to equate a good or bad dancer with how they did in bed, but Henry blew that idea out of the water.

With her back pressed to Dark and Yummy's chest, she felt the warmth of his breath on her ear. She was too close. She was starting to feel stirrings of longing in her belly and tingles in her panties, and it felt wrong. If Henry walked in, she knew he would be hurt, and she didn't want to hurt him.

Since when did she think about what would or wouldn't hurt one of her hookups? But Henry wasn't just a hook up to her. He was more. Aubrey's body stopped moving altogether when realization fell on her. She had fallen for Henry and denying it was useless.

"I'm sorry, I have to go." Aubrey extracted herself from Dark and Yummy's arms and ran for the door.

Chapter Twelve

The walk home was not nearly as calm and relaxing as she had hoped. Knowing that she had fallen for Henry scared the crap out of her. What if she screwed this up, too? What if once she gave in and was no longer fighting it, he got bored? But at the same time, that didn't seem like Henry at all.

At a little strip mall on the same street as her apartment was a comic book store. She never really paid it much attention before, but seeing it made her smile. She should really go in and see if there is a little something she could get Henry as a thank you. Maybe she just wanted to go in because it made her think of him.

She rolled her eyes at her antics. She really was that girl, after all. Damn him and his 'dig deep and let me in' ways. The little bell rang as she stepped in, and the two people in the shop looked up at her. She must have looked a mess after work all day then the bar, but neither said a word. They just watched her for a moment before returning to their comic books.

A little door opened behind the counter, and a short man with red hair and freckles came out. He looked to be in his twenties and he greeted her. She looked around the room, a bit at a loss. She had no idea what was good or bad, or if Henry even needed any of it. Aubrey walked up to the counter and saw the name tag on the man's shirt. Carl.

"Um, Carl? I was wondering if you could help me out. I'm looking for a little gift for someone to say thank you, but honestly, I wouldn't know one cape from another."

"Not a fan, are you? Not a problem. What do they like?"

That was a good question. Henry wore all kinds of superhero stuff. She hadn't noticed if he wore one design over the others. "I'm not really sure. He wears a lot of superhero clothes, though."

Aubrey pointed to a few familiar symbols on nearby books, and Carl took note of them.

"Do you know what kinds of collections he has? Or wants to start?"

Again, a question she didn't know. She sighed and felt horrible. She didn't know Henry at all. In all the time they spent together, she hadn't asked him a single thing about what he liked or read or anything. She had every opportunity and never took it. But then again, it could lead to shop talk and that was still off limits. She wasn't going to jeopardize her job.

"Look, I am the worst person in the world for not knowing this stuff when I know it's what he loves. Hell, it's what he does, but I have no clue. He lives around here, maybe you know him. Henry Maximus?"

"Henry? Yeah, I know Henry. Everyone who comes into this place knows who he is. And he does shop here, but never in person. He goes by the online store. He would be mobbed if he walked in here. How do you know Henry?"

Aubrey just looked at him and cocked an eyebrow. Did he not see her? How else would a hot woman know him? But she better be the only one shopping for him. Then she stopped. Was she really that superficial?

"Right. Never mind. Let's see. He pretty much has everything for his Superman collection—" Carl stopped talking and his eyes widened. Turning rapidly, he started mumbling to himself and searching through boxes under the counter. When he popped back up, he held a comic book in his hand. "This! I just got it in and 'hadn't put them out on the shelves yet. It's not too pricey but I know he will want it if he sees it."

"How much?" His comment on it not being pricey made her think that's exactly what it was. To her, it just looked like a few pages of a filled in coloring book. She would never say it out loud, at least not in the store... or around Henry, but how expensive could it be?

"Seventy-five. And only because it's for Henry."

"Seventy-five dollars for a comic book? Seriously?"

"Yes. Seriously. It's a collector's edition, and that's cheap."

"And Henry will like it?"

"Absolutely. I will even wait a day or two to put it out, so you have a chance to give it to him."

Aubrey thought about the bills coming up and what was currently in her bank account. Then she thought about Henry's smile, and how she could use the comic book as not only a thank you, but as a gateway into a conversation about him.

Good relationships were all about trying to make each other happy and getting to know each other, and she wanted to really try to make this one work. She was succeeding at a job finally, why not a relationship?

"Okay, I'll take it."

~*~

Aubrey could hear the arguing before she opened the door. Her night had already been a long one, and she did not want to have to listen to the insane arguments of a fifteen year olds relationship.

She placed her key in the door and opened it to her brother and Mackenna standing in the middle of the mostly empty living room. A box was at one end of the room and pieces of metal and cloth were strewn about. Both were red faced and held angry stares but neither said a word.

"Okay, then. I'll be in my room." Aubrey quickly made her way passed the angry pair and went straight to her room. Once the door closed behind her, the shouts started again. Apparently, Mackenna had spent the little money they had on a couch, and the mess she had just walked through was how Ben had thought they decided to save it for baby stuff.

Turning the television on and plopping down onto the bed, Aubrey took her shoes off. When the shouts got louder, she turned the television up. When that didn't work, she knew she had to intervene or the neighbors would be calling the apartment manager. Then she heard a thud and a shatter.

Aubrey clicked off her TV and flung her door open. "HEY!"

Both fighting teenagers stopped and looked at her. "Mind your own business, Aubrey!"

Mackenna was walking a damn fine line. Aubrey took a deep breath to keep from shouting back and said, "If I get one complaint about this noise, you two will have to find somewhere else to go. I am trying to help you out here but I will not deal with this crap. Couples fight, but screaming is not okay. Grow up. If you two decided on saving the money, Mackenna you are wrong. If there was no discussion, and it was Mackenna's money to begin with, Ben you're wrong. It's time to grow the hell up. That means talking shit out with your significant other. Not having screaming matches, and for crying out loud, stop throwing shit."

"Like you know what it means to grow up. You haven't been able to leave the house for more than a few months at a time. It's the only reason we're here. You need us to keep this place and to feel like an adult. Well, let me tell you something, you are not my mother. You are my roommate, and you don't get to tell my boyfriend or me what to do. You won't get to tell our child what to do, either."

Mackenna stood with both hands on her hips and a glare in her eye. Who was this girl? Aubrey had never seen this side of her before. Was this the girl her parents wanted to keep away from Ben? If so, she really couldn't blame them.

"I don't respond to petulant children," Aubrey said then turned to Ben. "I think this mess needs to be cleaned up, the fighting needs to stop, and the two of you need to talk this out without yelling. I don't care how you figure it out, but this won't continue. Oh, and the way she was speaking to me, won't happen again, or she won't have a place to live. Got it?"

Mackenna's eyes widened in shock and Ben just agreed. She was all for helping them, and continuing to help Ben and the baby, but she wouldn't tolerate Mackenna's temper tantrums any longer.

"Oh, and how is the job hunt going?" She asked before walking back into her bedroom.

"I put in applications at a few places on the way to school, and I have a few more to fill out and take back tomorrow," Ben replied. She was proud of him. He was taking this curveball his life threw at him with a real grown-up approach. He hadn't complained once and had done everything Aubrey had asked of him.

"Mackenna?"

"I'll get to it. I was sick before school and tired after. I am pregnant, after all."

Aubrey just shook her head and closed her bedroom door behind her. Plopping down on her bed, she buried her head in her pillow and screamed. Her voice was muffled by the fabric, and it's a good thing too, after telling the two teenagers in the next room that screaming wasn't the answer to anything.

She wished she had Henry's number. She wanted to talk to him. She needed someone to talk to about the terror that was currently still arguing with her brother in the next room. Had she jumped too soon when inviting them to live with her? *Probably.*

Aubrey scrolled through the contacts on her phone. Not one of them did she feel like calling to talk to about this. Her parents would just pull the 'I told you so' card. Three of the others were random hook-ups that put their number into her phone that she never deleted, and then there were work numbers.

Sadness crept into her heart. Henry was right. She didn't let anyone in. She was lonely and it sucked. A lot. A tear fell from her eye, but instead of wiping it away and pretending it never happened, she let it roll down her cheek and drip onto her pillow. Proof that she did have feelings and that a crack was forming in her hardened shell that protected her from everyone else.

Aubrey's phone rang out loudly with the beep beep beep of her alarm. Sitting up, she wiped the sleep from her eyes, and then turned it off. She didn't remember going to sleep, and when she looked down and saw the same clothes from the day before, she knew she had fallen asleep while contemplating her own loneliness. She huffed to herself. *Pitiful.*

She wondered how she would get in touch with Henry. Although, if things kept going the way they had been, he would find her first. A smile played at her lips as she thought about how he kept finding ways to run into her.

Aubrey showered and dressed for the day and headed out of the apartment a full twenty minutes before normal hoping to get coffee and see Henry in the process without being late to work. She left the comic book wrapped safely in the plastic and tissue paper nestled inside of the box that Carl had placed it in with such tender care. She had to stifle a giggle at the idea of the comic book being treated like a glass vase.

Aubrey had already made it halfway down the apartment hallway when she heard a door open behind her. She quickly looked over her shoulder to see her brother running toward her in his pajama pants. He still hadn't put a shirt on, and his hair was a disaster. She stopped walking and turned toward him, waiting not so patiently. She didn't want to miss her chance at seeing Henry.

"Hey, sorry, but could you pick up some milk on your way home? Mackenna has been craving cold cereal at all hours, and she finished it off last night. She is going to be seriously cranky today without it."

"Not that I mind, but why can't you get it on your way home from school, which if you forgot starts in an hour."

"I actually got a call a minute ago for a job interview. I don't even remember applying, but hey, maybe it was one of those online job search things I put my information on."

Elation flooded through her. She was so proud of him. He was really trying to do the right thing and had grown up in a way that she was just figuring out. "Ben, that's great! Where is it?"

"This coffee cart thing in one of the big buildings. I have the address, but can't remember now. I know it's just making coffee but—"

"No buts! It's a first job, and it's better than nothing! They know about school and will work around it?"

"Yeah, the lady said that they like hiring high school students to help teach them work ethic before the 'real world'. I wanted to laugh and say 'Lady, this is real world for me' but I didn't. Figured just thanking her was better."

Aubrey laughed and nodded her head in agreement. "Absolutely better. I'll get the milk on my way home, but I might not get here till after dinner. I'm presenting a huge idea today to Mike, and I might have to stay late if he wants me to help implement it."

"Okay, I will tell Mackenna. If she has an issue, she can take the bus to the store and get it herself."

Aubrey just closed her lips into a tight smile and nodded at him. She wouldn't open it and say anything about Mackenna. She wanted to. There were so many things springing to mind in that moment, but none would actually help. What was the saying her mother used to say all the time, if you don't have anything nice to say, don't say anything at all.

"Okay, I need to get ready for school, and you need to get to work. Good luck with the big idea thing. Keep your fingers crossed for me."

Aubrey made a big show of crossing her fingers for him. He laughed and ran back to the apartment. Shaking her head she turned and went down the stairs. A smile lit her face as she opened the walking gate that kept her apartment complex nestled away from the busy street. Leaning up against a black town car was Henry with two coffees in his hand and a smile on his perfect face.

"Hey," she said, a little softer than she had intended. Recognizing the flutters in her stomach as more than physical longing had made her lose her confidence. She was a bit shy and nervous around him. She took a deep breath and stepped forward.

"Hey," he said back and stepped toward her. Standing on the sidewalk, they stared at one another. Neither was quite sure what to say. Aubrey didn't know how to talk to him now that she actually had real emotional feelings for him, and from the looks of it, he was waiting to take her lead. "Is that for me?" she asked, pointing at one of the cups of coffee in his hand. He laughed and stepped closer, handing her the hot cup.

"Sorry, yes, it's for you. Can I walk you to work?" Henry had a hopeful look in his eye but his normally cool and calm demeanor was fidgeting. Could she make him as nervous as she felt?

"I would like that." She smiled at him, and the two walked side by side in a quiet, comfortable silence all the way to her building.

Chapter Thirteen

As her building loomed into view, she knew her time was coming to a close with Henry. They hadn't said a thing since he handed her the coffee, which he somehow got perfect without ever asking her what she drank, and that was okay. She didn't need words to feel close to him, but all of a sudden, it felt like wasted time.

"There's my building," she said pointing at the almost skyscraper just a few building in front of them.

"Yeah, I guess it is."

"I was thinking last night about how I don't have your number."

"Did you want to call me?" he asked with a cocky grin.

"No!" She said out of habit. She shook her head, irritated with herself for constantly pushing him away, even when she knew she wanted him closer. "I mean, yes. I wanted to talk to someone about my horrible argument with my brother's girlfriend, and then realized that the only people in my phone either were work related or people who just wouldn't care. I knew you would."

"Tell you what, give me your phone number and I will text you later today. And you can tell me all about your brother's girlfriend."

She smiled at him while rattling off her number. He cared. Her heart swelled while a nervous and terrifying energy flowed through her with the thought. She knew he would care, and suddenly, the fact that Mackenna was the wicked witch didn't bother her so much. She knew Jenna would be waiting to complain about something upstairs, but that didn't bother her much either. What mattered stood in front of her. And he looked at her as if she had hung the moon.

Aubrey leaned forward and kissed Henry on the cheek, simple and chaste. But the heat she felt through her lips, and when his hands gripped her waist, made her want so much more than chaste.

Henry pulled her body flush against his and wrapped his arms around her, cocooning her in his warmth. His hug was better than any other... and for a hug, that said a lot. She tucked her head into the crook of his neck and breathed him in. All too quickly, he let her go and stepped over to the curb where his town car was waiting.

She gave him a little wave and opened the large glass door. After stepping inside, she fought the urge to turn around and look at Henry one more time. She made it five steps before she lost the battle. She whipped around just in time to be rewarded with a killer smile and a little wave before he disappeared into the car.

~*~

"Mike, don't you see? The best way to market the old games is to make them new!" Aubrey said with exasperation. She had been pacing his office for ten minutes going over every bit of research and dead end ideas she had come up with in the search for the perfect plan. So far, he wasn't as excited as she was.

"That wasn't what I asked you. I said we needed to market the old games, not make new ones. Aubrey, can you please just focus on the job I gave you?" Mike was sitting at his paper covered desk with a waste basket full of coffee cups and another full one on his desk. He looked tired, and his hair seemed to have a touch more grey than what she remembered.

"I know. You asked for a way to market the titles in the envelope. You wanted an idea to make the companies resign with Viola. This is it. We keep everything about the games the same. We just need to make them playable on the new platforms. We can call it a retro line and offer it to all the clients, eventually. How many parents out there used to play these games but don't have a system anymore? They have the newest system for their kids. These games will give them the chance to play the game they loved on the system they already have."

"And what about the majority of the market? Why would they want to play these games?"

Aubrey pointed to the stack of papers she brought in. They were print outs of the forums where the kids were saying how great the story lines sounded. "Look, they are interested. As for the graphics, if we market it as retro and get some musician or hot actor to play it since a lot of them remember these games, then the kids will follow."

"Huh," Mike said as he looked over the papers in front of him. Aubrey could see the wheels turning in his head and started to get excited. "How much would it cost to make one game playable on all platforms?"

"I am still putting numbers together for that, but it will be less than half the cost of a new game because the story line and graphics are already done. It's just in the coding to make it playable, then the marketing campaign, which I have ideas for as well."

Mike and Aubrey spent the next four hours huddled away in his office going over the entire plan. By the time their stomachs began to grumble, Aubrey was pretty sure that Mike was going to green light her project. She was proud of herself. All that was left was to pitch it to the company on the first of the month. That meant they had three weeks to perfect everything.

The two left the office with smiles on their faces. Mike kept his as he headed for the elevator in search of food to sop up the copious amounts of caffeine in his stomach, but Aubrey lost hers the moment she saw Jenna leaning against the wall with a sour expression on her face.

"You two seem mighty cozy in there. Give up on the billionaire and decide to make your way to the top one boss at a time here at Viola instead?"

"What the hell is your problem? We were working. The walls are glass, for crying out loud."

"You didn't deny it."

Aubrey couldn't believe the audacity of her. Her mouth dropped open and quickly shut.

"What was it, Jenna? Was it how I always made sure you were on time for every meeting? Was it how you had your entire week scheduled perfectly, or how I kept your notes and ideas from going into the realm of insanity? Or was it how all the time I was your assistant that I never once let you down? Which of these *horrible* things made you decide I was your enemy?"

"Like you don't know. I thought you were the perfect assistant for so long. But all you were after was a promotion. Apparently, you got tired of waiting and had to make me look bad. You had to throw your ideas out there when that isn't your job, and you had to kill any chance I had of making this company a ton of money just so that stupid woman would tell Mike that she didn't want me to handle her company business, but you."

"What the hell are you talking about?" Aubrey honestly didn't have a single clue what was going on. What woman? She never tried to make Jenna look bad. She managed to do that on her own. Aubrey was always the one smoothing things over so that she didn't look bad.

"Oh, like you don't know. The contracts came through last week, and Leslie Hunter specifically asked that you run lead."

Aubrey was dumbstruck. Why hadn't she been told? She never intended to take anything away from Jenna. She was trying to help her and smooth things over like she always did. She handled Leslie no different from any other client. But maybe that was the problem. Leslie was different. They had a heart and money weren't their sole interest.

"I didn't know," Aubrey said as Jenna stormed off. She didn't even give her a chance to explain. She was intent on believing that Aubrey was a she-devil out to steal her job. For the first time, Aubrey believed that she was good enough for Jenna's job. But she didn't want it. She liked being in market research. She excelled at creative ideas. Schmoozing people wasn't her thing. She could do it, but she wanted to be more than the pretty face who entertained company. She wanted to be the one coming up with the numbers. She wanted to be the one coming up with the campaigns. Jenna could keep the fancy dinners and business meetings all over the country. She wanted her little apartment, a little office, and enough time at home to really be with Henry.

Her cell phone alerted her to a text. Knowing it was Henry before she even pulled the phone out, she smiled.

Hey beautiful. Save my number and you can call me whenever you want.

She read the text a handful of times before responding. He called her beautiful. Not sexy or gorgeous or anything else. Beautiful. She hadn't been called beautiful in a very long time. There was something special about that word that no other physical description held. It made her feel special. It made her truly feel beautiful.

Saved. I think I just might have to do that.

She saved his number into her phone and thought about calling him right then and there but decided that it might seem a little desperate. The phone pinged in her hand.

You want to call me now, don't you?

Her mouth dropped. How did he know? She looked around quickly wondering if he came into the building to surprise her, but he was nowhere in sight.

I was thinking about it. How did you know?

She waited for his response. And waited. And waited. But it never came. She sighed and headed to the little cafe the building put in a few years prior to grab an apple or a banana and a bottle of water. She was going to work through her lunch, but she needed something to tide her over until dinner.

Aubrey sat at her table in the abandoned office just as she had the day before. She poured over numbers and graphics and looked through the list of celebrities that the company had contracts with. After an hour, her eyes were beginning to cross. The information she needed was right there in front of her, but putting it all together was harder than she thought. Every other time she gave her ideas over, she just handed the data she had found on their database over to the person leading the team. This time, there was no team and she was the lead.

She had a new respect for Donna and Jamison downstairs.

Leaning back and closing her eyes, she reached up and pinched the bridge of her nose before rubbing her eyes. When her phone rang out in the silent room, it startled her, causing her finger that was soothing the sore muscles around her eyes to slip and poke right into one.

"Damn it!" she yelled before answering the phone. "Hello?"

"Aubrey? Did I catch you at a bad time? I can call back." Henry's voice flowed into her ear causing her to smile despite the burning sensation in her cornea.

"No, not a bad time. Just hurt myself. I'll be fine. Promise. No need to call back."

"Not another coffee incident, is it?" She laughed and said no, telling him what she had done. "Then it's my fault, and I have to make it up to you. How about dinner tonight? I can pick you up from your office."

That sounded wonderful but having the CEO of the rival company walking into her building might not go over so well. "How about you meet me outside? I just—"

"No need to explain. I get it. I will be waiting outside for you. I hope you don't have plans tonight. We aren't eating in the city."

"We aren't?" she asked in a little whisper. Excitement raced through her. Where was he taking her? Was it a surprise? What if it were horrible? She could fake it, of course. She stifled a giggle. She was good at that even if she rarely did it. If the guy sucked, she refused to make him feel like he didn't. But she cared if she hurt Henry's feelings, and she knew that at least she wouldn't have to fake it in bed.

"Nope. Got this huge thing coming up and the tabloids are everywhere. I figured we would escape the madness. Just you and me instead of you, me, and a dozen flashing cameras."

"That sounds like a good plan then. I never thought in a million years that would be a dating problem," she laughed. Only, he didn't laugh back.

"I'm sorry."

"Henry, there is nothing to be sorry about. We will go and eat wherever you are comfortable. It's okay. Really."

"Does six work for you?" he asked. His tone still hadn't gone back to the cheerful one that they started the conversation with, but at least he wasn't apologizing for things out of his control.

"Six is perfect."

They hung up, and Aubrey got back to work.

The minutes ticked by agonizingly slow. Aubrey felt like she could have gone from one end of the city to the other in the amount of time it took the clock hands to turn from five twenty-five to five twenty-six.

A knock at the door made her jump. Looking up from her piles and piles of papers sitting before her, Bridgette stood in the doorway of the empty office with two coffees in her hands and a smile on her face.

"Hey, so Mike's been pretty happy with whatever it is your doing up here. Told me I should see if you needed some coffee. And well, I know you, and the answer to that question is always yes."

Aubrey could smell the wonderful aroma from across the room. As if it beckoned her, she stood and walked straight over. Taking the steaming mug from

Bridgette's hand, she took a sip. She closed her eyes and sighed. It was perfect.

"Yes. You are one hundred percent right. The answer is always yes," she laughed and motioned with her head for Bridgette to follow her back to the table. "So Mike is happy?"

She was fishing for information, but she couldn't say she was sorry. With the way Jenna had been acting, and the lies she was telling him, she wanted to make sure her job was secure.

"Yes, very. He thinks whatever you're working on is going to save this company from losing some big players. So big he won't tell anyone what it is, so it doesn't get leaked. I don't even know."

Aubrey automatically felt a sense of pride, and a need to cover her work on the table. Almost as if Bridgette sensed the change, she laughed and shook her head.

"Don't worry, I won't look. I just wanted you to know how top secret he is keeping this. I know how badly you want to move up here. I get it. I just want to help you get there."

"Don't you want to move up?" Aubrey asked, almost shyly. She didn't want to offend Bridgette, but she couldn't imagine wanting to be an assistant forever.

"No, I like my job. Viola pays me well, I get to travel around with Mike three times a year, and my schedule lets me have both a professional life and a personal one. Mike isn't like Jenna. I am his assistant, not his fallback for when he screws up. Jenna put a lot of her job on you. Mike doesn't. Now, if Mike gets a promotion, that is if this company survives the Maximus-apocalypse, I hope he brings me with him."

"Maximus-apocalypse?" Her heart sank. How could someone like Henry be at the top of so many people's shit lists? She couldn't imagine he wanted to put them out of work. She gnawed her lip in concentration before releasing it the minute it reminded her of Mackenna. Stupid girl. Carrying her niece or nephew. If she lost her job because Viola went under, what would happen with their apartment? Shaking her head to rid herself of the random thoughts, she looked back to Bridgette.

"What? You haven't heard that one yet?" Bridgette asked with a laugh.

"No, I hadn't." Only, Aubrey didn't laugh.

"What's wrong? Did I say something?" Bridgette had lost her sense of humor and became very serious watching Aubrey. Should she tell her? Maybe she would have some actual dating advice.

"I sort of have a date in twenty minutes."

"Oh, do you need me to get out of your hair?"

"No, it's just...well...um..."

"Just spit it out already."

"I kind of have a date with Henry Maximus." Aubrey waited for Bridgette's reaction, but the girl sat in front of her with a blank look, not saying a word. "Did you hear me?"

"Oh, my fucking god. Are you fucking serious?" Bridgette's voice was high pitched and got louder by the second. "Henry fucking Maximus!"

Aubrey wasn't sure if she was excited or angry, but either way she had to bring it down a level. "Hey, shhhhh!"

Bridgette immediately stopped talking but a smile lit her face, and she started bouncing in her seat. "That is freaking amazing!"

"So you aren't mad?"

"Why would I be mad? Maybe a bit jealous, but not mad! How is he, ya know?" she wiggled her eyebrows and burst into giggles.

"Because he is the Maximus part of Maximus-appocalypse. I thought everyone here would think I was a traitor. Jenna sure does."

"Oh, some might. But I don't care. I know you wouldn't sabotage Viola. You didn't answer my question."

A little ease settled into Aubrey, and she dished with Bridgette for a few minutes about the amazing Henry Maximus before excusing herself with a promise to call when she got home from her date. Maybe she did have an actual friend after all.

Chapter Fourteen

Aubrey stood in the lobby out of sight of the doorway with two minutes to spare. She had reapplied her lipstick and tried to comb through her hair with her fingers in the elevator on the way down. She was ready, but she didn't want to be early. Bridgette said to not look too eager. Heading outside before six exactly sounded eager, so she stood and waited. And watched the clock click over. When it finally hit six, she strode out of her hiding spot and toward the glass doors.

Only, she didn't see Henry's town car near the front of the building. Trying not to be disappointed, she opened the door and scanned the street. His town car was nowhere in site. Neither was his Mustang. Her heart sank into her gut. Had he stood her up? Of course, he did. She had nothing to offer him. She was right, she gave in to a date, and he lost interest.

Aubrey wiped away the single tear that escaped her eye and turned abruptly to walk home. How stupid could she have been? That's what she gets for letting someone in. Screw that and his stupid offer. He would never actually hold up his end anyway. Why would he?

"Aubrey!" a voice called from behind her. She stopped and turned to see a very tall man with dark glasses and very broad shoulders approaching her. He was intimidating, and she considered turning around and running the opposite direction. "Thank you for waiting. I apologize for not seeing you sooner. Mr. Maximus is waiting in his vehicle around the corner. He sent me to get you. I am the driver for the evening."

"Why didn't he meet me himself?"

"He didn't want to draw attention to you. He has been managing a rather large deal that will affect many corporations and reporters are everywhere. He also just got some other news, but I think that's best for him to tell you."

Aubrey took a deep breath and tried to decide if she should trust this man or not. Had Henry really sent him or was he some media person looking for an inside story? Had they been spotted together at some point?

"He said you weren't very trusting and to tell you the place he is taking you will let you order black coffee and toast at any time of night, so take all the time you need to decide to trust me."

She had to laugh. Yeah, Henry sent him. She just nodded and motioned for him to lead the way. The man walked back toward her building and across the street to a yellow SUV. She looked at it, then back to him, and back to the car. Why didn't she just guess the behemoth of a car belonged to the giant man?

He opened the front seat and helped her in. The car was spotless. When he slid into the driver's seat and started the car, he buckled his seat belt. Then he waited. And waited. And Aubrey looked around wondering why they hadn't left yet.

"Um, are we waiting for some code word or something?"

"Nope, I just want to make sure I get you to Mr. Maximus in one piece, and to do that I need you to buckle up."

"Oh," she said as she grabbed the buckle, "why didn't you say so?"

"I thought belt safety was common knowledge. I didn't want to insult you."

Irritated, Aubrey huffed. "Whatever, can we just go please?"

"Yes, Ma'am."

"Oh god, please don't call me Ma'am. I'm not old enough to be a Ma'am."

"Sorry. Would Ms. Vincent be acceptable?"

"What do you call Henry?"

"Henry."

"Why does he get such informal treatment while I'm Ma'am or Ms. Vincent?"

"He told me he would fire me if I called him sir one more time. Then he told me he would put my likeness into a video game if I called him Henry."

Aubrey laughed. That was a good bribe. Henry seemed pretty good at those. "So what game are you in?"

"Some new one coming out later this year. A Greek god or some such." Aubrey's eyes narrowed. Greek God? Had Maximus Gaming landed the game from Becca Stine?

"Greek, huh? Any idea what it's about?"

"No. Henry didn't specify. Just asked if I wanted to be a Greek God or a basketball player. I mean, come on. That's not even a question." Then he laughed a full on belly laugh—the kind that makes all the muscles tense up and release, and is so contagious that Aubrey couldn't help but laugh herself. Maybe this driver was okay after all.

"So, Mr. Driver, Where are we meeting Henry?"

"Mr. Driver?" he asked, shaking his head. "Henry is waiting over there, in his green pick up truck." Mr. Driver pointed to a fairly decent pickup truck with an extended cab and tinted windows just a block up on their side of the street. "Ms. Vincent, you can call me either Bruce or Mr. Post, if you prefer."

"Henry isn't the only one good at deals. You call me Aubrey, and I'll stop calling you Mr. Driver."

Bruce looked at her and smiled, nodding his head, "Deal."

Aubrey thanked him for the ride and hopped out of the SUV and tried to casually walk to the truck. Too bad every nerve ending in her body was alight with fire with every step closer to Henry she took. There was no way her strides were as cool and collected as she wanted them to be. She felt as if she were nearly running, her sights set on the truck that held Henry behind its dark glass. Surely, he was watching her, seeing her excited face, noticing how eager she was to reach him—watching her walk straight into a trash can.

The cool dirty metal of the can slammed into her thighs, causing her to jar forward, nearly falling into the receptacle. With a shudder of disgust and a soul-crushing feeling of embarrassment, she righted herself. Aubrey made eye contact with the truck, wondering if Henry sat inside in a fit of laughter.

Only, instead of having a moment to collect her thoughts and come up with an excuse as to why she walked into the damn thing to begin with, Henry's door opened and he jumped out, running toward her with a look of worry crinkling his eyebrows.

"Aubrey! Are you okay?"

"Fine, just embarrassed and feeling a bit gross." She held her hands up and looked down at her dress, which held a long line of something dark right where her legs hit the trash.

"Come on, let's stop and get you some clothes, and you can shower and change at my place before we head out for dinner."

"Your place?" she asked with a flirtatious smirk.

"Well, I would offer to take you to yours, but I don't want reporters camped outside your apartment. At least at my house we can drive straight into the garage and go into the house from there. No one sees you, so no one knows to follow your moves as well as mine." Henry led Aubrey to the truck and helped her in just as a flash of light went off.

"That would make sense then. And the clothes? Where will I get those? Do you also have a stock of women's clothes at your place? Perhaps items that the many women I am sure you had strolling through there left behind in hopes for a phone call?" Aubrey tried to keep things going as smoothly as before even though she spotted two photographers jump out from around a

corner as her door closed and take a few pictures of
Henry before he got in.

"You do realize there are roughly fifty women's
clothing stores between here and my house?" He
looked at her with worry, even if his words were light
and playful. She knew he was wondering how she
would react to the intruders.

"I don't know where you live." Aubrey decided to
just ignore them. They didn't matter. Henry did.

"Sure you do. I bought the house on the corner of
Frankfurt." His demeanor lightened up as he started
the truck and drove down the street.

"Frankfurt? As in the street two blocks from my
parent's house?"

"That would be the one. I told you I moved back
to town. I saw the house was for sale, and it's perfect.
Small and normal. Well, except for the fact that our
little small town is now swarming with cameras. The
coffee shop on main is pretty happy about it. I don't
think they've had so much business in years."

"But you could buy any house you wanted, and
you chose that little house on the corner of a small
town with little going for it? Didn't you want a
penthouse or a mansion with a million rooms and your
own theater? Isn't that the thing for big shots like
you?"

"I didn't grow up with money. I never had dreams
of making it rich. I wanted to make games. I got lucky
and happen to have a knack for business and have an
even better team working to make sure that the
company runs when I get tired of showing up to
meetings. I would much rather be in the development

room working on coding. I don't want what big shots want. I just want to work and be happy. Have you seen the tabloids? Money doesn't make people happy. It usually just messes everything up. All of my assets are in the company. I take a monthly salary to live on, and the company pays for things like Bruce to make sure I'm not mobbed, but I don't rely on it."

Aubrey was in awe. Not many people would have billions at their disposal and not plan on using it. He could live in the lap of luxury, and Henry wanted a tiny house on a quiet street in a small town. He wanted to work and be happy.

"That's pretty great."

"Seriously?"

"Yeah, I mean, it makes sense. You never know how long your business will be the top dog, and if you blow through your money, what will happen if Maximus Gaming folds? All those other guys would be living off a fast food salary, and you will have plenty of back up funds to find something that makes you just as happy."

"So what about you, what do you want out of life?" Henry asked her without looking away from the road. Henry checked the mirrors frequently, more often than most drivers would. After a few moments, his body relaxed. When Aubrey tried to slyly look in the side view mirror, she saw that no one was behind them. "They're gone."

"Sorry, I was trying not to mention it."

"I know. Does it bother you? It shouldn't be for much longer. The news will hit tomorrow, and then it will be insane for about a week, but I'm small potatoes compared to the actors in whatever new hot movie is coming out."

"If I'm being honest, it's a little strange. But I can handle a little strange. Oh, and to be a great Auntie. You know the type that the little bugger will love more than anyone else, someone she can look up to and talk to."

"Huh?"

"You asked what I wanted out of life. I want my life to be something that my little niece will be able to look up to. I want her to love me most of all and know that I will always be there for her."

"Did Mackenna have an ultrasound already? It's a girl?"

"No, but I just have a feeling. This sounds horrible to say, but that little girl is going to need some kind of female role model because Mackenna is just not gonna cut it unless she grows up."

"But what do you want for you?"

That was a really good question. Aubrey wanted the promotion at Viola. It was a job that paid well that she was good at. She wanted to be happy. But that seemed so generic. She couldn't say exactly what she wanted for her future beyond the promotion. Did she have no ambitions? Her life had always been about the now. She figured she would worry about the later...later.

"What everyone wants, I guess. Health, wealth, and happiness?" She knew it was a stupid answer. But saying she had no goals in life felt wrong. Embarrassing. Not good enough. Would she ever get to a point that she was good enough? She was even a failure at her own dreams and goals. She had none.

"That's a cop-out."

"I don't know what you want to hear, Henry. Not all of us have our lives as put together as you do."

"I didn't say you had to. But there has to be something you want out of life."

Aubrey sat silent for a few minutes as she watched the city slowly dwindle into suburbs then into the blank expanse that would lead to their tiny hometown.

"I thought we were stopping so I could buy something to wear. You plan on telling me where we're eating yet?" She thought a change of subject was a good idea. She hated that she was a failure at even knowing what she wanted. She couldn't do anything right.

"We are. There's a tiny shop that just opened on Brook Street, next to the bank. Real trendy stuff, or so I'm told. I have no clue about women's fashion. I'm lucky the comic shop has a stock of killer shirts." Henry motioned to his tee that had a giant green muscular man on it making a rather scary face. The words around it said 'You won't like me when I'm Mad'. Aubrey laughed. She couldn't picture Henry being mad. "And I may have also employed a personal shopper for work stuff."

Aubrey laughed and smiled, the sullen mood she was in forgotten. As the fields and trees began to thin, and buildings other than barn or farm houses came into view, Aubrey knew the craziness was about to begin.

~*~

To anyone else, the cars parked along the streets, and the ten cars waiting behind the only traffic light in their tiny town, would mean nothing. After all, that's typical for most towns. Just not small town. Small towns with one light and only a handful of streets with houses and school grounds that actually held all three schools behind a single fence didn't typically see any sort of traffic, unless it was game night at the high school or Sunday morning heading to or from church.

Aubrey watched as stranger after stranger climbed out of their cars with cameras and other electronics in hand. As the truck rolled down the street, and heads and cameras followed, she was glad that Henry had thought to get the tinted windows put in.

"Do you think you have a shirt and belt I could borrow? I don't think I want to get out with all of them to go buy a new outfit. You said we weren't going anywhere fancy, right?"

"Right. Yeah, you can borrow whatever you want. I am sorry about all this."

"It's pretty insane," Aubrey said as she watched one camera man running alongside the street holding his camera out and snapping pictures without actually looking at what he was taking.

Henry stayed quiet the rest of the way to his house. He pushed a button on the sun visor above him and the garage door opened. If he thought pulling in was going to be easy, he was wrong. The crowd of reporters stood in his driveway and refused to move.

They began shouting questions at the truck, not that it was easy to understand with everyone shouting at once. Not to mention being inside the truck and not daring to roll down a window.

"I think I am going to have to go out there and talk to them to get them to move. I am going to get out and walk toward the front door. When I get them clear, slide over, and then drive the truck in. I'll be in behind you."

"Okay." Before he could slip out of the truck, Aubrey leaned over and brushed a kiss across his cheek. She could tell that the attention and flashing cameras outside of the truck were bothering him. To be honest, it was a little intimidating. But she didn't want him to think a few pictures were going to scare her off. Especially, not after she finally accepted how she felt for him.

Henry gave her a sweet smile, a light dancing in his eyes that made her happy knowing it was because of her. His hand grazed her cheek before he quickly opened the truck door just enough to get out and keep her hidden away.

Aubrey watched as Henry led the mass of people away like he said he would. He walked over to his front door and stood on the top step. He spoke with his hands gesturing wildly. She watched as he held his audience captivated and wished she could hear what he said to hold their attention so raptly.

When his eyes locked with hers (intentionally or not, since she knew he couldn't actually see her through the windows), she remembered why he went out there in the first place. Quickly putting the truck into drive, she parked in the garage and closed the door behind her.

Aubrey opened the truck door and slid out. She wondered if she should go into the house or wait in the garage for Henry. She looked at the door that led to the house more than once as she perused the shelves that lined the cement walls.

There were no tools or yard stuff, no bikes or sports stuff, just boxes. Tons and tons of boxes. Each box had a white sticker on the edge pointing out with a hand written number on it. The boxes started at 1935 and went up through 1985. At least on the wall she was looking at. A quick look around showed her that the other walls held similar boxes. Before she had a chance to actually open one and see what was inside, the garage spilled with light.

Henry stood in the doorway, leaning against the frame with an amused smile on his face. "You can come in, you know. I didn't plan on making you wait out here all night."

"I didn't know if I should go in or not. I mean, it's your house, and I didn't want to intrude or anything."

"No intrusion, come on," he said with a jerk of his head toward the open door. Aubrey moved to the steps that lead into the house, following behind him.

"So what were in the boxes?" she asked, closing the garage door behind her. The kitchen they stepped into was very cozy. It had yellow walls and only one countertop that looked like it had seen better days.

"Comic books."

"All of them?" Aubrey stopped in her tracks and looked at Henry with shock. There were a lot of boxes down there. And they weren't little boxes. "Have you read them all?"

"Yeah, all of them. I have been into comics since I was a little kid. The ones out there either are damaged or just not worth much. I have a room set up for the special ones. It's temperature controlled and everything. Want to see?"

Henry's eyes were lit up like a kid on Christmas morning, and he was excited to see what Santa had brought. How could she say no to that? She had little interest in superheroes, but she had a ton of interest in Henry.

"Sure," she said. He grabbed her hand and led her through his little house. There was artwork on most walls, all of which was actually framed comic book stuff. Surprise, surprise.

"This," Henry said with reverence as he unlocked and opened a door in the hall, "is my comic room." He stepped in and waved his hand animatedly, beckoning her in. "Please don't take any out of their protective covers."

"I pinky promise. I will keep my hands to myself." She had to stifle a giggle. They were just comic books. Weren't they meant to be read? She didn't understand it, but she did see that it was important to Henry.

They spent the next twenty minutes wandering the small space. Henry pointed out special editions and figurines he had collected over the years, and finally, he came to a case against the back wall. It had its own lights and was sitting inside of a glass box. He stood before it with tears in his eyes.

"This one is the most special of them all."

"What is it?" she asked, in a hushed tone. She didn't know why, but it felt like a quiet moment was needed. The cover had Superman on it holding a car above his head and people running around him with looks of terror. In the corner, the price said ten cents. It had to be old.

"It's less about what it is, although, just owning it is a wet dream for every collector out there, but more about how I got it. It was an auction."

"An auction? How is that important?"

"Because the money went to the pediatric ward. This one comic was able to fund medicine for fifty kids for a whole year. Every time I look at it, I smile."

That warmed Aubrey's heart. Those kids got another year, their parents got a year without medical debt, and Henry got his comic book. "I bet they send you Christmas cards every year."

"No, actually. It was a silent auction. No one knows who won. I didn't want anyone to know where the money came from. That way, no one feels indebted to anyone. The kids get what they need. I know I helped where I could. Not to mention, I have the first ever comic book with Superman in it."

"You didn't want people to know you donated a lot of money to the hospital?"

"No. I didn't do it for publicity. I did it because it mattered. Those kids matter. My money? Doesn't matter. I have plenty and they don't. I can spare it. What I don't need are more reporters asking for more stories and interviews about what and why I spend my money. I would have just donated it, and have before, but I really wanted that comic book."

Aubrey was in awe of him. He was starting to turn red, blushing no doubt about wanting the comic book, but she saw nothing wrong with it. He had every right to that book. It didn't matter if he got something in return for what she was sure was a, generous donation. It was still a very good cause.

"That is really sweet."

"Do you just want to stay in for dinner? I can make something for us instead of going back out into the crazy that's outside."

"Sounds great."

Henry smiled at her and reached out for her hand. He gave it a tug before leading her out of the comic room and down the hall. He pushed open the door at the end of the hall to reveal his bedroom.

Aubrey smiled, knowing the reason she was in his room was actually quite innocent, but the thoughts swirling through her mind were far from innocent. In fact, they were quite sinful. She still wanted to prove to Henry that she was able to forgo sex in favor of a meaningful relationship. She could do it. She could.

"The shower is through there," Henry said pointing at a door on the far wall, "and there's my closet. Pick anything you want."

Henry left the room, closing the door behind him. Aubrey turned and took in his room. The furniture was all dark, and besides the stray comic books and novels laying on his night stand, it was pristine. The bed was made, there were no clothes strewn about. Giggling slightly at the idea that Henry might be a clean freak, she opened his closet.

His shirts were color coordinated, but only after they were superhero organized. Aubrey looked through them, not sure which one to pick. She knew a few of them, of course. She didn't live under a rock. Superman, Batman, Spiderman. Beyond that though, she was a little lost. Even though they were staying in for dinner, she wanted to look cute. She wanted Henry to drool when he saw her. So she flipped past the tees and grabbed a button down and one of his belts that hung from a hanger before heading into the bathroom.

Aubrey could hear Henry moving about outside the bedroom door. She smiled thinking of him, pacing and wanting. When she turned the water on in the shower to warm, she decided not to close the bathroom door. She felt like a vixen teasing him so, but if he were to peek into the bedroom, he would see the open door, and the glass shower, and would be filled with desire.

She knew they had a no-sex deal going on, but that didn't mean she couldn't entice him a bit, reminding him of her more sensual side, as well. Henry may want her to let people in and connect emotionally, and she knew he was right, but she felt the need to remind him how amazing the physical side could be, too. Didn't he crave her touch the way she did his? If not, he would.

Standing with her back to the open door, she began to remove her clothing. Slowly, she unbuttoned her shirt, exposing her lace covered breasts and smooth stomach, before slipping it off her shoulders and letting it fall to the floor. Aubrey took a glance in the mirror, which gave her the perfect view of the bedroom door behind her to see Henry standing there, watching her. She smiled a little at the hunger in his eyes.

Reaching behind her, she unclasped her bra, freeing her breasts, her dark nipples pebbling from the excitement of being watched. Aubrey licked her lips as she unzipped the skirt she wore and let it drop to the floor. The only time she looked away from the mirror was to drag her panties down her legs, bending over, letting Henry see her in all her womanly glory. Aubrey stepped out of the pile of clothing that surrounded her feet and opened the glass shower door. Steam billowed out, encompassing her in heat. It was nothing compared to the warmth that spread between her legs.

The hot water sprayed her, soaking her from head to toe. Aubrey could feel that Henry was getting closer. She wasn't sure exactly where he was, but a quick glance toward the door told her he was no longer in the hallway. Her heart beat faster, and the wetness between her legs was more than just the water flowing from the shower. Him being so close when she was so bare made her need that much stronger. Aubrey grabbed the washcloth that hung on a little hook under the shower head and lathered it up with soap. It smelled like Henry. Aubrey closed her eyes and inhaled his scent.

The cloth rubbed against her skin. It was rough, almost like she imagined Henry's stubble would feel like. A moan slipped from her lips as she grazed her nipple and pictured his mouth wrapped around it, teeth nipping at the delicate flesh.

A loud thud came from just outside the bathroom. Aubrey jumped in surprise from the noise. When she saw the shadow of Henry's figure dance across the floor in front of the door, she knew she had him. He was there, listening to her, wanting her. She wondered if he was touching himself as she was. She wanted him to.

Aubrey let her hand travel the expanse of skin to her pussy. Smooth and hairless, the folds between her legs were especially sensitive. She was so turned on that just the slightest graze sent waves of pleasure through her. Aubrey's back fell against the shower door as her fingers explored, bringing her closer and closer to the edge.

Images of Henry touching her, licking her, pounding his rock hard cock into her flew through her mind with every stroke of her fingers. The water pounding down on her, hitting her nipples in just the right way was an added bonus. The strangled moan she heard come from just outside her door where she knew Henry stood, cock in hand, sent her flying over the edge she had only thought she knew before.

Breathing heavily, Aubrey finished her shower as if nothing had actually just rocked her fucking socks off. Her face flushed when she shut the water off. She had to pull it together. She needed to dress and walk out of there as if nothing had happened. She needed to show him that she could be both. She could be the sexual being and emotional. She could let him in and let herself connect in both a mental and physical way.

Aubrey stepped out of the shower and dried off. She toweled her hair, so it fell in dark messy waves around her shoulders. When she pulled Henry's button up work shirt on, it fit exactly as she thought it would. The bottom of it fell to just above her knees. Aubrey fastened his belt around her waist and made sure the top three buttons were undone. His shirt made the perfect little dress.

Checking herself out in the mirror one final time, she left the bathroom and switched off the light, smiling at the memory of the best shower she had ever taken in her life.

~*~

As Aubrey walked through the house, a wonderful aroma filled the air. She had to close her eyes and inhale just to appreciate it completely. She hadn't eaten a real meal in weeks. With traveling for work, avoiding her parents for Ben, and moving out, her main meals included quick sandwiches from the deli near work, fast food, and twenty cent packages of ramen noodles.

"What is that amazing smell?" she asked as she rounded the corner to the kitchen. Henry looked up with a slight flush to his cheeks before directing his attention back to whatever was sautéing in the pan. Aubrey smiled to herself. He was just as affected as she was.

"It's asparagus risotto with Shrimp in a lemon dill sauce." Aubrey's mouth watered just listening to him. That sounded so fancy!

"You can really cook like that?" she asked in shock. Her mother always cooked from home, but it was things like meatloaf with mashed potatoes or spaghetti. Nothing as fancy as what he was making her.

"Yeah, I really can," he said with a chuckle. "I enjoy cooking. It's kind of a hobby of mine."

Henry plated up their meals and the two sat at his little table by the window. Henry watched as she took her first bite. She was pretty sure she moaned as the flavors melded together in her mouth. Embarrassed, she looked away quickly, but when she let her eyes drift back to Henry's, she saw how happy he was that she reacted that way. His eyes were lit up and a smile stretched across his handsome face.

"I'm glad you like it."

"It's amazing. Thank you."

"So, how goes things on the home front. I know you were having issues with the roommate situation."

"I hate the fact that I see my parent's point about Mackenna. She is not the person I thought she was. On the up side, Ben is really showing me that he can grow up. He is proving his responsibility a lot faster than I ever would have been able to."

"That's a good thing then. Is there a way to sit them down and talk to them about her behavior?"

"Without sounding like their mother? I don't know. I have no idea where to go from here. I told them in the beginning that they would both need to get jobs to help with bills and such. I wasn't asking for a lot, but I was hoping it would get them started with realizing their life won't ever be all about fun again. They won't be handed anything just because they ask for it anymore. They will be the ones doing the handing from now on. They can't be kids anymore. They will have their own to take care of. I think Ben really gets that, or is trying to at least. Mackenna just sees the pregnancy as another reason to get her way."

"I don't know what to tell you except that maybe you need to be the parent. They are still fifteen, right? I know you don't want to, but you might have to."

Aubrey sat silently for a moment, taking another bite. Henry was right, even though she didn't want him to be. She didn't want to be the one to lay down rules and enforce them. She didn't want to reprimand them or 'punish' the poor behavior. But if Mackenna didn't get it together and do her part, and that was a stipulation of living there, she would have to find a way to live somewhere else. The whole idea of being just like their parents and kicking her out made Aubrey feel like the worst person in the world. She knew it wasn't because they were stupid and had unprotected sex, but that didn't make it any easier. Not wanting to sour the mood for the rest of the night, Aubrey switched gears and changed the conversation.

"So, what happened after high school?" Henry looked up from his own plate of food in confusion for just a moment before evening out his expression. She hoped he understood that she didn't want to talk about Ben and Mackenna any longer.

"Well, during high school I was doing online college courses, so when we did graduate it only took me another year to get my degree. If you hadn't noticed, I didn't have much of a social life, so I could bulk up on classes and get it done fast. Most people thought I loved school because I got good grades. Truth is I just wanted it over faster. The more classes I took at once, and passed, the sooner I got to say goodbye to the whole thing."

She should probably have known that. She knew how badly he was treated. But like the self centered girl she was back then, she thought he liked school anyway. He was the geek after all, and to her seventeen year old brain, school work outweighed the bullshit her friends put him through. Thinking back on it, it made much more sense for him to despise it.

"I had no idea."

"Most people didn't. It's a geek thing, I guess. We are all supposed to like school and learning and all that. I must be an enigma." He laughed a little, but Aubrey could see the slight hurt in his eyes.

"Let's see, an extremely sexy man with a thing for superheroes and not spending money when he is probably one of the few people in the country who could do so without worry. Not to mention turning down hordes of women practically salivating at the idea of getting naked with you. Enigma is probably a good word." She smiled hoping he would see the lightness in her statement. It was meant as a compliment. She hoped he took it that way.

"I didn't turn you down," he said and moved closer.

"Oh, but you did. Quite a few times, I might add. I thought I had lost my touch."

"No, telling you no was the hardest thing I had ever done. You were like a dream come true, but I knew I couldn't just sleep with you. I knew my heart was involved. It's always been you, Aubrey. I never really knew you in high school, but you were the one girl I always knew I wanted to know. Every girl that passed through my bed after I made my business profitable, I compared to the idea of you. I had my fair share of women, but it was always just sex, and that got so lonely. I needed more, but the more that those women needed was money. I tried to actually date a few times, but it wasn't me they cared about. They cared about my wallet. It was easier to just turn them all down then be fooled again. Then I saw you in that bar in New York City. It was like it was meant to be.

"I had just been told about two more companies we landed, and I told my acquisition's guy I would take him out in thanks. The minute he let my name past his lips, the girls surrounded us. I had just enough liquor in me that I didn't care if they were money hungry. I could pretend they weren't. I could pretend it was actually me they wanted. Then you walked by.

"Those girls paled in comparison to you. When you took the drink but then ignored me, I thought for sure you knew who I was but were still too good for me. And then you left with that guy. I hadn't been so jealous since high school."

"Tall Hottie," she said with a grimace. It was the first time she had felt bad for taking a guy home. Not because she had sex with him, but because even though she didn't know him then, it hurt Henry.

"Tall Hottie?" he asked.

"Yeah, that's what I called him. No names. I don't do names with hook ups. It's easier to keep it completely physical." Henry's face contorted with his lip curling up and his brows scrunching together. It made her want to crawl into a hole. He was disgusted by her. She never understood why it was okay for a man to sleep around to get what he needed but so horrible for a woman? "What? You can have a past of sleeping around to get your rocks off but I can't? What kind of bullshit is that?"

"That's not what I was thinking."

"Bullshit. Tell me, Henry. At what point is it acceptable for me to sleep with a man?"

"No, really. I hate the thought of you with anyone else. I know you have a past. So do I. I hate that you thought you could only have the physical when you are worth everything. You deserve to have it all, Aubrey. You are one of those special women who don't need a man in her life, but deserves one. You can take care of yourself, and your brother, and your career, without the help of anyone."

"You think I like hearing my old boss tell me she slept with you years ago? This is why I don't like relationships, Henry. Feelings suck. You feel all happy and giddy inside until you don't. Eventually, the times you don't out number the times you do. What's the point?"

"The point is finding that person and working at a relationship to keep it from getting that way. Look at your parents. They love each and are still together after how many years? Look at your grandparents. And I hate to ask, but what's your boss' name?"

He had a point. But her family was the exception to the rule. She had never been exceptional at anything. Why would she suddenly start just because Henry had come along?

"Jenna. She said it was a few years ago. Trying to get secrets from you about your company but you wouldn't talk work."

"I am ashamed to say that I have no idea who she is. The name doesn't ring a bell. This is what I mean. I shared something intimate with this woman that I don't even remember. I hate that. The girls I attempted to date, I know who they are, but the others? I hope I would be able to pick them out of a lineup, but I can't promise you I could. You and I aren't much different, Aubrey."

"I guess not."

The room they sat in filled with silence. When their plates were empty, Henry stood and took their dishes to the sink. Aubrey hated that she felt so distant to him. Had they really just argued? They were barely in a relationship. At least they never had a conversation stating they were. But was it a deep conversation or an argument?

Standing, she walked over to him and stood at his back as he washed the dishes. Aubrey wrapped her arms around his waist and placed a kiss in between his shoulder blades. "Are we okay?"

"More than."

~*~

The ride home was less eventful. Aubrey held Henry's hand in her lap the whole way, and he explained the complexity of Marvel vs. DC. She wasn't sure she actually got it, but seeing him so excited made her happy.

Henry opened her door for her once they pulled up to her apartments. Aubrey looked up at him hopeful. She hadn't been so nervous for a goodnight kiss since her first date all those year ago. Henry's eyes darted from hers to her lips and back. When his hands gripped her waist, she stepped forward, giving him permission. Slowly, he leaned in and placed his lips on hers. Soft and sweet, yet much too quick. Even though it ended sooner than she would have liked, it was perfect, and she practically floated up to her door. Aubrey fumbled for her keys, lost in her thoughts of Henry and how even though their conversations weren't easy, she felt closer to him because of them.

The door in front of her wretched open. Mackenna stood on the other side in her pajamas—the same ones from that morning. Her hair was disheveled and her eyes were on fire, boring a hole into Aubrey's head.

"Where have you been? You were supposed to be home hours ago! Where's my milk?"

Shit, she forgot all about Mackenna and her damn pregnancy craving.

"I am so sorry. I completely spaced. I had a long day at work, then a great date," she said a little dreamy. Maybe she could share some girl talk and connect better with Mackenna. Maybe that would help them find a common ground. "I will get some first thing in the morning."

"I don't care about work or your date. You told Ben you would get me milk. Are you a liar now? Ben said how great you are for everything you are doing but I just think this is a way to get us to break up. We have fought more since you convinced him to move in here than ever before. It's you. You are doing it all. How the hell do you forget milk? You are doing this on purpose!" Mackenna was screaming, and Aubrey hadn't even managed to get in the door.

A few neighbors had opened their curtains or doors to see what the commotion was at such a late hour, and Aubrey gave them an apologetic look before practically pushing her way into the apartment.

"You need to calm down. I had no intention of causing any fights between you and Ben. I just didn't want him or my soon to be niece living on the damn street. I did forget the milk and I apologized. What more do you want?"

"Ben and your niece, huh? What about me? Don't care if I live on the street. I want you to get me my damn milk! I have been sitting here all day waiting for a bowl of cereal. It's the only thing I can keep down. You say you care about the baby so much, then why are you starving it?"

"All day? What about school?"

"How am I supposed to go to school if I haven't eaten? Gotta feed the brain and all that. It would be a waste of time if I didn't eat."

"Are you fucking stupid?" Aubrey yelled back. She finally had enough, and Ben took that moment to open the door.

"Whoa! Aubrey, don't talk to her like that!" He yelled, slamming the door behind him. He had only heard part of the argument, but what he did hear didn't paint her in the best light.

"Ben, she didn't buy my milk! Told me I didn't need it, and she wouldn't help me at all!" Mackenna cried, running to him. He wrapped his arms around her and kissed her head, glaring at his sister.

"I did not. Since when have I ever spoken to her that way? I apologized for forgetting and only called her stupid when she told me she skipped school. Look at her, she didn't even get dressed today."

"Mackenna? I thought you said you were helping the teacher during lunch when I texted you to find out where you were. You were here the whole time?"

"I couldn't go in! I was nauseous. This baby makes me feel gross. I just want him to grow and be big enough to get the hell out of me, Ben. I hate being pregnant."

"Maybe you should have thought about that before having sex," Aubrey mumbled, walking away from them. Ben shot her another glare, but said nothing.

"I know, but you have to go to school and look for some kind of job. That was the deal, remember?" Ben reached into his pocket and pulled out a bill. "Here's a five. Why don't you ask to borrow Aubrey's car and go get some milk."

The look Ben gave her told her he was trying. She needed to let the little bitch borrow her car. She rolled her eyes but grabbed the keys from the hook they hung on in the kitchen and held them out to her.

"But I can't go out looking like this! Can't you go? Or she can since she promised to get it anyway."

"No, you can get dressed or go like that, either way. You go and get an application at the same time. The grocery store would be a good place to work. They pay well and are part of unions. Pretty soon we are going to need those benefits they provide."

"Fine." Mackenna snatched the keys from Aubrey and stormed out. Ben just stood there and stared at her.

"What? You didn't hear the whole conversation." Aubrey was on the defensive. She didn't want to fight with Ben. She hated when they did, but she wasn't going to back down because of Mackenna.

"You didn't have to call her stupid. And why didn't you get the milk? It would be so much easier if we could just keep her happy."

"And what about you and me? Don't we get to be happy where we live, too? I had a long day at work and then a date, okay. I'm sorry I forgot, but I have a life, too."

"A date?" he asked, turning back into the brother she knew and loved. The one who would talk to her about anything.

"Yeah, his name's Henry," she said. The two of them sat down and talked about her night, leaving out the more intimate aspects, of course. Ben was happy for her. And dying to see the comic book room.

Chapter Fifteen

When Aubrey awoke the next morning, she felt lighter than she had in a while. Perhaps the night with Henry had changed things, or maybe it was finally reconnecting with her brother. The fight with Mackenna was far from her mind, even after she stormed back into the apartment a good two hours after she left, without milk, and headed for her bedroom without a single word to Aubrey or Ben.

Ben said his goodnight, knowing he needed to deal with his own relationship, and Aubrey hugged him before heading to her own room. The night had it's lows but they paled in comparison to the amazing highs it had. She finally had it together.

She dressed quickly, almost knowing that Henry would be outside waiting for her. The thought alone made her smile. She shook her head at her own train of thought. There she was, the self proclaimed barfly who only needed a good lay once in a while, ready to jump head first into a relationship. And she didn't have to give anything up to get it! How had she gone so long believing she had to choose one or the other?

Aubrey ran out the door with a quick wave to Ben and Mackenna (who was actually dressed for school) and headed for the street. Standing at the gate was Henry, coffee in one hand and a paper in the other. He wore a worried look and her steps faltered. What had happened since they said goodbye just the night before?

"Tell me," she said as she approached. She just wanted him to spit it out. She opened the gate and reached for her coffee. Henry leaned in and pressed a soft kiss to her lips, surprising her. It was daylight, and he was openly kissing her? She didn't mind, but he had been so careful.

"Apparently, we made the paper. Here," he said and handed her the paper with the headline *Maximus Gaming Buys Out Bennette Industries.* She looked up, shocked, but confused as to why this affected her.

"Bennette? That's why everyone is swarming?" Bennette was Viola's big competitor before Maximus Gaming showed up. Maximus and Bennette together would be huge. They would be a super power in their own right. Viola didn't stand a chance. All Aubrey could see was her future with the company being torn away if she couldn't manage to convince Buffet, Hodges, and Keith that they loved her idea. They had to stick with Viola, with her idea.

"Yeah, but flip the page." Henry bit his lip and pushed his glasses up, looking away as she turned the page. There, at the top, was a picture of Henry helping her after she fell on the street. And another of her in his truck. And another that was somehow taken through the window of his house at his dinner table. They were looking at each other with smiles on their faces. The bold print on the page sent a shiver through her. *Could the Most Eligible Billionaire be Taken?*

"Okay then, so what now?" she asked, almost afraid he was going to tell her to take a hike. He didn't seem like the type to actually enjoy being in the spotlight and there he was with two articles about him. Because of her.

"I guess that's up to you. Am I taken?"

"Do you want to be?"

"By you? Absolutely."

Aubrey didn't answer him. Instead, she threw herself into his arms and kissed him. She kissed him with such passion that she heard a few gasps from strangers walking by and a cat call coming from a passing vehicle. But none of that mattered. Henry Maximus was hers. And she was his.

When they broke apart, he smiled down at her. And nodded with his head in the direction they had come to walk each morning. With their fingers entwined, they smiled at people who pointed and waved as they held their own copies of the morning paper. Aubrey thought she saw a few cameras flashing but ignored them. If Henry 'weren't going to acknowledge them, neither would she. As they passed the comic book store, Carl was just opening the doors. He waved at them and gave them both a thumbs up. Aubrey had completely forgotten about the comic book she had bought for him.

"Hey, after work you want to go to the bar? I feel like dancing." She did feel like dancing, but more than that, she wanted Henry to walk her home so she could surprise him with his gift.

"That sounds like a plan."

~*~

The entire floor was in a frenzy when Aubrey stepped off the elevator. A breeze whisked by her where a person used to be, papers scattered the floor and the shouts and arguments echoing off the walls were enough to send Aubrey directly into panic mode.

Aubrey quickly made her way over to Mike's office and Bridgette's desk. She had a pile of papers on her desk and a phone balanced between her ear and her shoulder while her hands furiously typed on her computer.

"What the hell is going on around here?" Aubrey asks.

"Buffette sent word to not bother with a presentation. After seeing the paper this morning, they feel safer going with Maximus. Now a good amount of other clients are worried about the merge affecting them. If we go under, how and what protections do they have in place. It's a disaster. Oh, and I want details later." Bridgette gave her a wink then started talking on the phone about meetings with a different client, reassuring them that Viola is still hard at work for his firm.

Mike opened his door and called her in. Sitting there were the CEO of Viola, Jenna, and two other people that she wasn't quite sure who they were.

"In here, now." Aubrey did as she was told and walked in, only to have the door closed behind her. She should have paid more attention when she approached Bridgette. If she had just looked, she would have seen the whole group and ran the other way.

"What can I do for you?" she asked, looking between them all.

"Aubrey, due to recent events, and news hitting the papers before we were aware, Mr. Fredrickson would like to hear what you have so far."

"I thought you wanted to keep that between us until it was ready?" she asked in almost a whisper.

"Well, things have changed, haven't they?" His eyes told of his disappointment in her. Of course, he had seen the pictures of her with their biggest competitor. But was her dating life really their business? They didn't talk about work. She would never do that.

"Look, Henry and I—"

"Maximus Gaming is our biggest competitor and they just got bigger. I need one hundred percent transparency on any possible strategy that is going to keep us in business. Mike seems to think you are the key to that. So please, do explain." Mr. Fredrickson was scary when he was angry, and she could tell he was angry. His brow was furrowed, his grey eyebrows almost touching each other, his eyes narrowed. When he spoke, it felt as if icy daggers were being thrown her way.

"Okay, let me go get my files," she said, glancing around the room. Jenna had a smug look on her face and rolled her eyes.

"Should we really trust such an important project to an assistant? She needs her notes to even tell us anything about the plan," Jenna said, looking to her colleagues around the room. Aubrey wasn't sure why she was even there. This wasn't a new company to acquire, but an old one to keep.

"Now, now, Jenna. Mike put his trust in her. Let's give her a chance." Mr. Fredrickson gave her a fond look and a pat on the hand. Jenna beamed up at him with doe eyes and a nod. Of course, she found her way to the top. Just like she tried with Henry. Aubrey shook her head and swallowed down her nerves.

"No, she's right. I had just wanted to give you exact numbers and projected dates of completion, which I don't have memorized, but I can give you the basic plan."

Aubrey took the next twenty minutes going over the remarketing of the old games, the reformatting of the programs, and the basic money structure. The men in the room sat silently, watching her as she finished. Jenna, on the other hand, scoffed.

"That has to be the worst idea I have ever heard. Kids don't want old games. You should have focused on the old guys. Get them interested again. Maybe do an auction for a few old systems to get the interest back up."

"Actually, Jenna, that would only gain attention for a brief period of time, and then we are back to square one. This method opens us up to doing the same for all of our clients and brings in a whole other revenue source." Aubrey was proud of herself. She watched as the men nodded along with her.

"Aubrey, this is a great idea. Get on the phone and set the meeting up with Keith and Hodges, and the sooner the better. Rough numbers will be fine for this meeting. We just want them to know that we are prepared and won't let them regret sticking with us."

"Yes, sir!" Aubrey left the office before anything could change. Now, if only she could get to them before Henry's team did. She just hoped that he didn't hold it against her when her proposal kicked his company's ass. Aubrey smiled to herself and found a quiet place to make the calls.

While she waited on hold with Keith, she typed out a quick text to Henry.

Apparently, dating the competition makes people nervous around here.

It only took a moment before he responded. Aubrey quickly tapped the screen to read what he said.

I hope it doesn't cause problems.

Aubrey didn't have a chance to respond because the head of contracts for Keith came to the phone. They were quite happy to hear that Viola was being proactive and coming up with a marketing plan for the old games, as well as the new. They were more than happy to set up a meeting for the following morning. Aubrey sighed in relief as she hung up. Scanning through the files on the computer, Aubrey found the contact number for Hodges. She knew their games. They would be a harder sell to the public, but with some creative marketing, she was pretty confident that her sales tactic would work for them, as well.

She punched the number into the phone and once again was placed on hold. She waited for five minutes. Then another ten. Finally, the phone picked up. It was the same woman's voice that put her on hold to begin with.

"Ms. Vincent? I am so sorry you had to wait so long, but Mr. Calhoon is busy. He is going to have to call you back."

"Oh, that is perfectly fine. Please have him call me at his earliest convenience." Aubrey rattled off the phone number and extension to the phone where she sat and just hoped that they did get that call.

Aubrey sat in her chair and watched the phone for an hour. She pulled out some files to work on, trying to get the numbers closer to exacts than estimates for Keith. She wanted to wow them, and everyone at Viola.

Quite a few people had walked by her, staring and whispering. Finally, someone got brave and walked straight up to her.

"So, when Viola goes crashing down, I guess you have a great back up." She knew people would think something like that, but hearing it out loud bothered her. A lot.

"That has nothing to do with it. I am doing everything I can to help Viola."

"Oh, so that's why you're sleeping with Maximus. Getting his secrets then?"

"NO! Henry has nothing to do with anything work related."

"Yeah, right," they said then walked off laughing.

Remembering Henry's text, she pulled out her phone. Irritation radiating off her, she typed out a reply.

No, no problems at all if you don't count basically being called a whore.

Henry's response was immediate.

How the hell did they come to that?

She scoffed at his naivety.

They think I'm with you as a backup for when Viola closes because you keep taking our clients.

I know that's not why. And so do you. Does their opinion matter?

Of course not. But damn it. I do have to deal with these people.

Aubrey noticed he didn't comment on the fact that Maximus Gaming kept taking Viola's clients. Perhaps it was a lapse in thought but what if it was on purpose? She typed another text before he could reply.

And what about the clients? Is it on purpose? Are you trying to close Viola?

There was no response for close to five minutes. With every second that ticked by, Aubrey got more agitated. Finally, her phone pinged.

I'm not taking them from you. Maximus Gaming, a company, is doing business and offering clients what they want. Viola, a company, has been old school for far too long. They need to update their marketing to keep their clients. Nothing is on purpose to close any business down.

Aubrey thought about that a moment. He was right. Up until they had brought her in, all of the marketing had basically been the same thing for each client depending on genre. All the sports games got the same treatment, just as all the fantasy games did. Nothing was new and exciting. Until they started asking for her ideas. As Mike said, they needed someone to think outside of the box.

Sorry. It's been a rough morning here. Still on for tonight?

Of course. I'll see you at six.

Aubrey put her phone away and waited a bit longer for the phone to ring. When it didn't, she took her lunch. Waiting outside the building was a handful of people with cameras and tape recorders. They screamed all kinds of questions at her. Everything from what was her name to what kind of underwear did Henry wear.

They swarmed around her, coming closer and closer. Fear encased her when they wouldn't let her pass. Her heart pulsed until a loud voice boomed over everyone, and they backed away, allowing her room to breath.

"Aubrey, come on. Ignore their questions. Just keep walking." Bruce stood beside her giving her enough of a shield that the media dare not approach.

"Thank you," she squeaked. Was this how it was for Henry?

Bruce walked her to the deli then back again. He handed her a card with his number and told her to call him when she needed to leave, at least until the media circus died down. She thanked him again and went back to work.

Unfortunately, the call came when she was out. And it wasn't good. They lost Hodges, too.

~*~

The rest of the day took a nose dive. People either avoided her like the plague or wanted to know every detail there was to know about Henry. By the time the clock struck five fifty-five, Aubrey was running for the exit. She just hoped that Henry was ready and waiting for her.

The lobby downstairs was eerily silent. The security guard that sat in the lobby with all the computers was standing with one hand on his baton and the other holding his cell phone. As Aubrey approached, she saw why. Outside their doors, a horde of photographers and news crews waited. She thought she glimpsed Henry's town car behind them all. She sighed loudly. She would be glad when the craziness was over, and they could go back to the way it was before the stupid merger.

"Sorry about that, Nick. As soon as I leave, they probably will, too."

"Don't you worry about a thing, Ms. Vincent. Do you need me to walk you to the car?"

"You might need to. But let me make a call real quick. More than likely, Henry has his driver with him. Those camera people seem to be a bit afraid of him. He introduced himself as a driver, but by the way people scatter when he is around, I'd call him a bodyguard."

Nick laughed as she pulled out her phone and dialed Bruce. What shocked her was after she hung up, the crowd outside went a crazy. Cameras flashed and people were shouting, and they all moved away from the doors, forming a tight huddle near Henry's car.

A few moments later, the doors opened and Henry stepped through with Bruce. She smiled at him and shook her head.

"You didn't have to get out."

"What kind of man would I be if I didn't come to the door to pick up my date? The secret's out. No way was I letting you fend off the wolves alone."

Aubrey kissed his cheek and turned to Nick. "If you want to deal with that insanity, we would appreciate it. If not, I don't blame you a bit. You might start getting treated like I have all day if they think you're helping the enemy."

"Don't you worry about that. Let's go." Nick walked forward and opened the door to the mad house. Henry grasped her hand in his and kept her tight to his side.

"Are you two an item?" one reporter called out.

"Is that a baby bump?" another yelled. That stung. Aubrey stiffened by his side before continuing to walk.

"Where did you meet? Is it a coincidence that you work for competing companies? Are you after his money, Aubrey?" The questions were flying a mile a minute. Aubrey barely had time to breathe let alone answer a single one. She kept her head up though. There was no point in hiding. Henry was walking tall, proud to have her at his side. She wouldn't cower away because the press was intimidating.

"Aubrey and I went to high school together. We reconnected recently and are a couple. Now, we will be on our way. Put a call into my firm to set up an official interview about the merger if you would like." Henry said it all with such grace and strength. He didn't stumble once or blink an eye. It was like he was meant for the spotlight.

She looked up into his eyes and smiled, willing him to feel the pride radiating off her. He smiled back and led them to the car. The questions didn't stop, but they didn't answer anymore. It took Bruce a minute to thank Nick for his help and to actually get in the car, but once their door was closed, the sounds of the crowd faded away and it was just the two of them.

In the car where they'd had mind blowing sex. Aubrey looked around then back to Henry with a devilish grin.

"They can't see us in here."

He just laughed. "So, with what just happened... do you still want to go to the club?"

Aubrey smiled. "This is where my contacts come in rather handy."

Aubrey pulled out her phone and called Kevin, her bouncer buddy. A few quick words were exchanged and she had gotten them back door access and gotten anyone with a camera or microphone on the banned list for the night.

"It won't stop them all, but it will certainly help."

"I never thought I would be grateful for any ex of yours."

"Not an ex. Just a buddy."

"Still. He saw you naked. That's enough to make me not like him."

She just laughed and smacked his chest before cuddling up to him. The silence was relaxing, and the warmth of his arms around her felt amazing. Just before they pulled up to the back parking lot, Henry kissed the top of her head, and then began to shift around.

Aubrey sat up and looked at him. He was fidgety and seemed nervous. Just like he had that morning.

"What's wrong?"

"I just never thought the beginning of us dating would be like this. I swear they only get this way when money becomes a huge issue and when I was put on that stupid eligible bachelor list. I promise it will go back to normal soon."

"It's okay. It's part of dating the city's most eligible bachelor, right?" She had been joking, but the look on Henry's face told her he didn't find it all that funny. "Look, I have gone so long failing at everything. Work, home, guys. I finally find myself in a position where everything is working. Everything is going right, and I don't want to let some stupid bitch with a camera ruin that. I really like you, Henry. That's not going to change because someone wants to take our picture."

"Someone? Try thirty someone's if I counted right back there."

"That just means we have thirty pictures to collect tomorrow to add to a scrapbook," She never thought she would be the one reassuring him. Henry was powerful and successful and for whatever reason, absolutely terrified she was going to bolt. "I'm not going anywhere."

"Okay. Let's go in."

The club had been busy. Aubrey and Henry got lost in the crowd and even if someone had managed to get past Kevin, they never found them. Sweat trickled down Aubrey's body as she pulled on Henry's hand, leading him off the dance floor and over to the bar where they ordered a couple drinks.

Henry's hands gripped her hips and pulled her roughly to him. He trailed his mouth from her shoulder up to her ear where he nibbled and licked at her lobe. Goose bumps covered her skin, and she shivered under his touch. Reaching up, she turned his head toward hers and kissed him. She took control, teasing his lips until he opened for her, wrapping her tongue around his, and pulling on his hair until he moaned.

"I'm ready to head home, what about you?" she said in his ear after breaking their kiss.

"Absolutely." Henry replied before pounding back the shot he ordered. Aubrey did the same, and then let him lead the way to the back of the club to leave the same way they came in.

Aubrey fumbled with her keys, trying to keep her lips on Henrys. She needed to get the damn door open but she couldn't part with feeling him against her. Finally, he pulled away and smiled at her.

"Open the door, Aubrey." She smiled back and turned around to open the door properly. She let Henry in, and then closed the door behind them. She held a single finger up to her lips to quiet him. She didn't want Ben or Mackenna to come out.

Aubrey took Henry's hand and led him to her bedroom, much like she did the first time she lead him to the dance floor in the bar. Once in her bedroom, she closed the door and pinned him to it, kissing along his chest and neck. Aubrey undid each of his shirt buttons agonizingly slowly, letting her tongue trace the opening until she dropped to her knees in front of him.

Undoing his belt, without taking her eyes off his, she licked her lips. She could feel him shaking beneath her touch and his hardness straining against his slacks. Just before she reached into his boxers to free his dick, he placed his hands on her arms.

"Aubrey, wait." She was completely startled and a little hurt by the tone in his voice. It sounded like he didn't want her—didn't want her to make him feel good. Swallowing hard, she went to move, but he didn't remove his hands, so she looked back at him.

"What is it?" she asked a tremor in her voice.

"Are you sure you want to do this? There's still two months left of the deal." Aubrey could see concern etched all over his face. She was almost offended that he thought she was in it for the cash, but after everything he revealed the night before, she could understand.

"Are you crazy? Of course I do. I was never going to take your money anyway. I just wanted to prove a point, but you proved yours instead. Now, can I suck your cock?"

Henry groaned then removed his hands from her arms and let his head fall back against the door. Aubrey pulled his length from his boxers and stroked the smooth skin once, twice, a third time before plunging him deep into her mouth.

Aubrey bobbed her head on him, taking him as far in as she could, and used her hands in rhythm with her mouth on the part that wouldn't fit. After a minute, Henry pulled her off him, hunger in his eyes.

He pulled at her shirt, lifting it up and over her head in a single swoop. We walked her backwards to her bed until her knees hit the edge and toppled her onto it. Henry removed his shirt before climbing on top of her. He lavished her neck and chest with his tongue, only stopping to pull the cup of her bra down to free her nipple.

Quickly, he sucked it into his mouth, nibbling ever so slightly before licking away the sting and sucking again. One hand massaged the other breast while the other hand found its way under her skirt and played with the edge of her panties.

Aubrey moaned at his slight touch. Her body was aflame with need, begging to be touched everywhere. She pushed up on his shoulder and he sat back. Aubrey sat up and unhooked her bra and tossed it to the side before shimmying out of her skirt.

When she lay back down, Henry just kneeled before her, drinking her in. His perusal made her pussy ache. She reached down to stroke herself, but he stopped her. Instead, he dipped his own finger into her wet folds. Aubrey's eyes closed on their own accord, needing to cut off her other senses to feel more.

When the pressure of his hands retreated, a warm wetness enveloped her. She looked down to watch him devour her, his hands kneading the flesh of her thighs. A building of pressure began in her belly and moved outward, making all of her muscles tense up until a final nibble on her clit sent her nerves into overdrive. Aubrey cried out in pleasure, her body shaking from the high. She gripped at his shoulders, clawing at him, trying anything to pull him up so he could fill her with his cock. But he wouldn't budge. His continued ministrations of the tongue sent her body into convulsions, and just when she thought she couldn't take another second, he plunged his fingers deep into her.

The scream that shot from her sounded inhuman. Henry pulled back, licking his lips with a smug smile on his face. Once Aubrey caught her breath, she leaned up on her elbows and watched him. She scooted herself further back onto the bed, all the while Henry crawled up over her, aligning himself with her.

With his eyes locked on hers, he used one arm to prop himself up and the other to guide his length into her opening. Henry thrust forward with a strength and speed Aubrey wasn't expecting. And it was amazing. She began lifting her hips in rhythm with his, forcing their hips together with such passion she was sure to be sore later. A good kind of sore.

Henry's hips slowed and his lips descended on hers. His lips were hesitant, teasing almost. He pulled back slightly to look into her eyes again, and she could see so much shining back at her in them. She could feel so much more than just his body doing wonderful things to hers. She couldn't voice it, or even think the words herself, but she knew that he could see everything in her eyes that she saw in his.

Chapter Sixteen

Henry had left sometime in the middle of the night. He woke her with a soft kiss and said goodbye before slipping out. He had hoped it would have curtailed the media circus surrounding her building the next morning. He was wrong.

Ben and Mackenna were plastered to the window, peeking out of the blinds when Aubrey came out of her bedroom. Almost simultaneously, they looked at her.

"What? Do I have something on my face?" she asked, feeling herself reddening. They had to have heard her the night before. They were going to tease her over her activities, she just knew it. Neither said anything. Instead, they pulled the curtain back slightly showing the horde of reporters outside her apartment door. "How did they get in here? What happened to the security?"

Before Ben and Mackenna had a chance to ask anything, there was a knock at the door. Aubrey approached it slowly as if it were going to fly open at any moment. When she pressed her eye to the peephole, the breath she didn't realize she was holding released and her muscles relaxed.

Quickly, she opened the door just enough to let Bruce's muscular frame through the door. The cacophony of noise shocked her. At first the questions were directed at Bruce, which he ignored. But the moment they realized her door had opened, they switched gears and were all about her and Henry.

When the door closed, the sound died down, but she could still hear the shouts from beyond the door.

"What the hell is going on out there?" Aubrey's voice was a higher pitch than normal. She began pacing the room, back and forth, back and forth. Tears prickled at her eyes but she was afraid to let them fall. What if someone got a picture of her crying? What kind of story would they spin with that one?

"One of the richest men in this country announced to the whole world that he was no longer the most eligible bachelor. He did this right outside your work. His biggest competition. It is a little disconcerting business-wise, and the media is looking for any story they can get. Henry sent me when he saw the news crews outside the building this morning." Bruce spoke as if this were routine, as if he were used to this kind of reaction. As if her whole life hadn't just been turned upside down.

"So when will they go away?" she asked almost in a whisper.

"When they get their story. You and Henry need to address them together. Right now, they are looking for anything to make a story out of. A baby bump, a ring on your finger, another man in your life." Bruce looked over to her little brother. A shudder ran through her that he was going to be pulled into the craziness.

"So Aubrey is dating someone famous?" Mackenna squealed. "Who is it? An actor? Musician?" Mackenna had jumped up and a light danced in her eyes. She was excited about the insanity outside their modest apartment. All Aubrey wanted was for it to go away.

"A billionaire," Bruce said. "Henry Maximus."

"Henry? The guy who lived a few blocks over?" Ben asked, finally speaking up. Aubrey had told him about Henry but never really told him everything. She just nodded. She didn't know what to say at that point. What had happened? Just a few days before no one knew who she was. No one cared who she dated. Besides a once in a while mention in the paper about Maximus Gaming, she hadn't even known what the owner of the damn company looked like. She had thought that since the merger was over, everyone would lose interest. She was wrong. So very wrong.

"I know he moved a while ago. And I think his 'parents moved, too. Otherwise, we would have heard about the famous boy from the neighborhood about a million times by now," Ben said.

"Yeah, they moved a couple years ago. I used to walk their dog to make money when I was like ten or something. I was so angry they left, and I couldn't find anyone else to pay me to walk their dogs. Their son was making a ton of cash, and they should have just given me like an envelope full of money to make sure I had enough for the rest of the summer. So selfish." Mackenna rolled her eyes and went back to the window. She started waving and smiling at all the cameras outside.

Aubrey could tell that Bruce was going to say something but she just shook her head. It was not the time to point out what a little brat Mackenna was being. From the looks of it, Ben was just as astounded by her words. She had never seen him look at Mackenna that way before—with such disappointment in his eyes. He used to think the girl hung the moon, Aubrey was pretty sure he was beginning to see that Mackenna wasn't who he thought she was.

"Hey, Aubrey, did I ever tell you what building I work in?" Ben asked randomly.

"No, why?"

"Oh, because I work at the coffee cart in Maximus Gaming."

Aubrey turned, her eyes narrowed. Maximus Gaming? He had to be kidding. Had Henry gotten him the job? She took a deep breath. She had to think. Was she actually mad at Henry for helping her brother out, if that is, in fact, what he did, or was she just irritated because of everything else? If he had gotten Ben the job, was it really a bad thing? No, of course not. But not telling her when she was worried about him and everything? Again, there was nothing to be upset over, even if she would like to have known.

"Well, that's a pretty big coincidence." Aubrey didn't want to tell Ben of her suspicions, but the fact that Bruce wouldn't look her in the eye told her all she needed to know.

"Ms. Vincent, if we don't leave soon, you will be late for work. My advice to you would be to not answer anyone's questions. Wait until you and Henry can sit down and talk about what gets revealed and what doesn't."

"Okay. Let me just grab my things," Aubrey said, not even bothering to correct him in calling her by her last name. She began gathering her briefcase and cell phone and a light jacket, almost methodically. So much was going through her mind, but mostly she wanted to make sure that Ben and Mackenna were able to get to school. With the way they stayed glued to the window, the press had to have seen them. "Bruce, after I get to work, can you make sure they get to school without being harassed?"

"We'll be fine!" Mackenna practically shouted. Aubrey huffed her obvious disagreement, and Bruce actually chuckled.

"Yes, I will come back for them."

"Keep the door closed until Bruce comes back. And don't talk to anyone, okay? I'm sorry you have to deal with this. I had no idea things would get this way."

Ben walked over and hugged her. When he kissed the top of her head and said it would all work out, she squeezed him tighter. She was supposed to be the one comforting him. He should be either freaking out or super excited. Wasn't that the standard reaction? She may not agree with Mackenna's antics at the window, but she knew they were normal for a teenager.

"Okay, let's go." Aubrey pulled out of her brother's embrace and looked to Bruce. He would be her shield. Even though she didn't know him well, she knew that he would protect her.

The door opened and Aubrey placed herself behind Bruce. She took two fistfuls of his jacket and stuck close to him. She could feel the bodies press in on them the minute they were out in the open. Everyone was shouting questions so loud and so quickly that they all blended together in a blanket of noise, none of which she could actually make out.

The steps were difficult to navigate holding onto Bruce like she was, and the elevator was not an option as there were another dozen reporters standing guard. Quickly, Aubrey released Bruce's jacket and ran down the steps next to him. On the third to last step, a single rock rolled under her foot and sent her crashing forward.

Instead of hitting the ground like she had prepared for, two strong arms wrapped around her middle and righted her. On shaky feet, and even shakier breath, Aubrey turned to thank Bruce. His stony face shocked her, until a dozen flashes went off, catching her off guard—and still in his arms.

Pulling away quickly, Aubrey resumed her position behind him, hiding her face from anyone's lens. Thankfully, the town car that Bruce had brought had tinted windows. Once she slid inside, she could actually breathe. She could still see all of them, but she was hidden from the world.

In the silence and privacy of the back seat, Aubrey let the tears fall.

~*~

The scene outside Viola wasn't much better. Aubrey had made sure to wipe her eyes and used a little compact she kept in her purse to freshen up before exiting the car. She made a beeline for the door, and thankfully, the security at the office was much better than at her apartment complex.

Aubrey looked at her watch and quickened her steps. She had five minutes to get upstairs and into the conference room. Five minutes to mentally prepare herself for the most important meeting she had ever had, or could ever have. She didn't know why they were risking everything on her, but she didn't want to let them down.

The elevator pinged, the doors opened, and Aubrey stepped out of the dark cart into the bright hallway filled with people. Everyone looked up and watched as she moved closer to the conference room doors. The skin on her neck prickled with every whisper that followed her. Uneasy nerves flared up, taking on the shape of a million angry butterflies fighting to the death inside of her stomach.

Mike stood by the door, pacing. When Aubrey approached, he looked up and relief flooded his face. "Oh, thank God! You are cutting it close, aren't you?"

"Sorry about that. Getting here was something else this morning." Aubrey didn't want to go into detail. Chances were he already knew about her love life, just as the rest of the nation if they watched the morning news.

"Are you sure you are up for this? I mean, you have the presentation ready to go, don't you?" Mike began chewing on his lip, and Aubrey could practically hear his heart thrumming in his chest.

"Yes, Mike. I do. I am ready. I can do this." She knew her words were full of confidence… if only she were, too.

"Okay, they're waiting."

The door opened and Aubrey felt a whoosh of air pass by her. She closed her eyes for just a moment to relax and zone in on the moment. Nothing outside of that room mattered in that moment. What mattered was the presentation she was about to give and to get the contract signed before they walked out of the room.

Aubrey stood at the front of the room with at least two dozen people watching her every move. She saw a few skeptical expressions pass over some faces and the others were stone. With every display she put up on the screen, with every figure she gave out, she lost more and more confidence in her idea. Not one smile or head nod in the bunch. She didn't know what she did wrong. When she came to her conclusion, the group from Keith stood abruptly.

"Interesting presentation. We had hoped for a more... unique idea."

"I'm sorry?" she asked, completely confused. She had given them that. Hadn't she?

"We had a teleconference early this morning with another company, and they had the exact same presentation. Down to the figures and regions to begin the plan in. If you can not find a way to honestly represent us, we will go elsewhere."

Aubrey stood at the front of the room, speechless. The men from Keith walked out without another word, and all eyes from Viola were on her. She swallowed back the knot in her throat and waited for someone to say something.

"How could you?" Mike asked, rage clearly in his voice.

Aubrey shook her head and tried to speak, to deny she had done anything wrong, but she wasn't given the chance.

"You have just condemned this company to death. The jobs of those two thousand people out there? They won't have them in another six months unless something big turns this company around. That was supposed to be this meeting," Mr. Fredrickson seethed. He picked up the conference phone from the center of the table and punched in a number. Aubrey looked around the room, hatred flying at her from all directions. There was one smug smile in the room. Jenna.

"What did you do?" she asked. No one seemed to hear her but the wicked witch from the west.

"I didn't do a thing. You, on the other hand, told your little boyfriend your plans, and he ran with it. How does it feel to be used? To be treated as nothing more than a means to an end?"

"You're wrong."

"Security will be escorting you out of the building. I never want to see you in here again. Your final pay check will be mailed to the address on file." Mr. Fredrickson said, then turned his back and left the room, the rest of the big wigs in tow.

Aubrey collapsed into the nearest chair, completely confused. What the hell had just happened?

She pulled her phone from her pocket while she waited for Nick to come and collect her. Quickly, she typed out a message to the one person she probably shouldn't.

I need you to come get me.

Henry responded almost immediately.

I will be there in five minutes.

Chapter Seventeen

Nick stood quietly in the elevator with Aubrey. She couldn't look anywhere but the floor. If she looked up, and saw the look of pity that she was certain was staring back at her from the security guard, it would all become real. Hell, the minute she stepped off the elevator, she knew that it would be a slap in the face how real it was.

"Ms. Vincent, for what it's worth, I don't think you would ever sabotage Viola." His words meant the world to her. At least someone believed in her. She had expected to hear from Bridgette at some point before being escorted out of the building, but she didn't. Maybe she hadn't built a real bond with her after all. She had thought she made a bond, a friendship with Bridgette. She didn't think she could feel any worse than she had when she was accused of sabotage of an entire company, but knowing that the one friend she thought she had didn't care enough to say goodbye hurt so badly she thought an ice pick was being stabbed through her heart.

"Thanks, that means a lot."

The elevator lurched to a stop as a ping bounced between the walls, alerting her to the insanity that was about to ensue. Nick held the button that kept the elevator doors closed. Aubrey looked up and nodded, letting him know that she was ready. Even if it was a lie.

They were able to take a few steps out of the elevator before anyone noticed them. It started with a single reporter who walked over calmly with his camera guy. She could see him looking back at the masses who, unlike him, were not paying attention.

"Aubrey, why were you fired? Are you a mole for Maximus Gaming?" The microphone was stuck out in her face, and the bright light of the camera felt like one of those interrogation room spot lights. What she wanted to know was how they already heard she had lost her job.

"Move aside, please," Nick said as he pushed passed the reporter. Aubrey didn't answer his question just as Bruce had suggested. Unfortunately, Nick's voice carried in the echoes of the lobby of Viola and that caught the attention of the rest. For the second time in a little over an hour, Aubrey was surrounded by people shouting at her, wanting to get her picture.

She couldn't handle it. Too much was happening too fast and she had no clue what to do. She stopped walking and held up a hand, waiting for everyone to quiet down. She only wanted to speak once. It took a few moments, but eventually, the reporters got the hint and stopped shouting over one another.

"I am not going to answer any questions. I am not going to be followed and harassed. I will call for the police, and I will have restraining orders placed against every one of you and your companies if I have to. Henry already made a statement about our relationship. That is all you need to know. Now, if you will excuse me, I have to go." Her voice wavered and she knew that her eyes must have been brimming with unshed tears as she spoke. Her hands were shaking, and all she wanted to do was crumple to the ground and cry but she refused to give them anything else to talk about. She had to hold it together just a little longer. She just had to find Henry.

During her little tirade, Aubrey saw the town car show up outside the doors. She knew that Henry was inside. If she could just get to the back door and slip in, she could find out what the hell was going on.

Too bad the reporters were not pleased with what she had said. Instead of backing off as she had hoped they would, their questions just grew in intensity. Instead of asking if she were a mole, they asked what kind of charges Viola would be pressing for selling secrets and breaking the confidentiality agreement all employees must sign. Instead of asking what brought her and Henry together after so many years, they questioned her fidelity.

Aubrey tried to get to the car on her own, but it became impossible without actually laying hands on someone. The town car's door opened and suddenly, Aubrey was forgotten. Instead of Bruce getting out and helping her into the car, Henry got out and distracted the reporters. He exchanged a quick look with Nick, who then grabbed Aubrey's arm and lead her around to the other side of the car. By the time she was getting into the back seat opposite Henry, the information-crazed group barely noticed her. The few who couldn't get close to Henry tried to get her attention but she ignored them. With her door firmly closed behind her, Henry said goodbye to everyone and got in himself.

"Well, that was a first," he said a bit awkwardly. "I am so sorry, Aubrey."

"What the hell happened?" Her voice was low but filled with ice. She was scared and angry about the way her morning started, she was confused and hurt with what happened at Viola, and she was just plain irritated with the circus that was currently outside of the car. It should have been an amazing day. It should have been filled with stupid giddy smiles and a pleasant soreness between her legs with a want for more. Instead, she was bombarded with bullshit.

"I don't know. I didn't expect this," he said, with a sweeping motion of his hand to outside the car. "I knew that the merger would have people following me, but I have never had them worry about who I date before. I hope you know how truly sorry I am. If you don't want—" he stopped talking, a catch in his throat. Aubrey could see the concern and worry in his eyes. What she didn't know was if it was for her and the life that had basically crumbled in the past hour, or for him—thinking about losing her.

"They are only half of it! What the fuck happened with Keith? I know I didn't tell you anything. How did you find out our pitch? How did you get our exact numbers? Please, tell me that this whole thing wasn't about growing your pocketbook and getting back at me for the stupid horrible shit I pulled in high school." She hadn't even considered it until it came flying from her mouth. Blinking back tears, Aubrey turned to look out the window at the city blurring past her window. If that had been his game, he did a hell of a job. Maximus would be the only big company in the gaming industry left, and she was utterly humiliated and heartbroken.

"Listen to me," he said sternly. When she didn't look, he put a finger tip to her chin and pressed, encouraging her to look at him. She complied, fully aware that her eyes were shining like wet glass with unshed tears. "Please, don't cry. I don't know what happened with Keith. All I know is that we had a meeting scheduled for this morning. I wasn't even there. I rarely am anymore. And no, this, you and me, has nothing to do with work. But I will find out what happened, and how we gave your presentation before you. I promise you that. As for the media circus out there, I don't know what is going on. We can keep a low profile for a while and hope they go away, or we can talk to them when we have all the facts of what happened."

"Viola fired me, Henry. Do you know what that means?"

"That they are idiots?"

"That, too," she said with a slight smile. The first one since the insanity had started. "What it means is that I have an apartment with a ton of bills, one pregnant roommate who has yet to get a job or even attempt to, and another who works at a coffee cart. How the hell are we going to afford to stay? I should be used to it by now, though. It's the way my life goes. Always has and apparently, always will."

Aubrey's head dropped into her hands and she breathed deep. Wiping her eyes before she sat up, she simply said, "Okay, new plan. Get home, talk to Ben and Mackenna when they get out of school, and get a new job. Quickly. If that fails like everything else, I guess my parent's attic is still up for grabs."

The tone of her voice held no real hope. That was because she didn't have any. She knew that she was being dramatic, people lost jobs all the time. But how many of them lost their jobs with reporters following their every move and had a brother with a baby on the way that they needed to make sure were taken care of?

"Don't worry, we can figure this all out."

Easy for him to say. He didn't have to worry about money or about losing a job he loved or about being called a mole and a whore in the papers.

Aubrey used her cell to call ahead to her apartment building. If there were still a horde of media, she would rather keep driving in circles. Thankfully, the apartment manager apologized for the earlier display of lack in security and assured her that the problem was taken care of.

Outside of the apartment gates were still swarms of reporters with cameras, but behind it, not a single one. The town car was let in, and the gate promptly closed behind them, allowing Aubrey to breath easier. They were actually going to be able to walk without incident up to her apartment.

Bruce opened the door but declined the invitation to come up with them. He said something about errands and to call if they needed to go anywhere.

Henry thanked him and Aubrey gave him a hug. He awkwardly patted her on the back before pulling away.

Henry took her bag from her and linked his hand with hers, leading her up the stairs to her apartment. There were no reporters, but the sheer number of eyes staring at them from behind curtains as they passed by was enough to set off Aubrey's irritation again.

Her fingers clenched and unclenched, and she would have little left of her teeth if she didn't stop grinding them. It was only the wince she happened to catch on Henry's face that made her stop.

"Sorry," she said, lifting his hand to see if she broke the skin with her fingernails.

"It's okay, I understand. Come on, let's go in." They had reached her door. Aubrey unlocked and opened it, letting Henry in. She turned and glared at what most would consider nothing but an empty corridor, but she knew behind each stupid curtain, a neighbor saw the look she was sending out. She hoped they were all ashamed of themselves.

Once the door closed behind her, the weight of the day over took her. She didn't want to think or do anything. She knew there were a million things to think about and plan and do but she was exhausted. Kicking off her shoes, she walked across the room, grabbed Henry's hand, and led him to her room. Once her bedroom door closed, she stripped down to her bra and panties and climbed into her unmade bed.

Looking up at Henry, she patted the bed next to her and turned on her side, curling into a ball with the covers pulled tight to her chin. She heard the rustle of his clothing and felt the dip in the bed when he joined her.

"Aubrey?" he asked gently, a slight sound of worry in his voice.

"I know. I just need to sleep. Sleep with me? Just for a little while?"

"Okay, for a little while." He kissed her shoulder and snuggled close. The warmth that he provided when he wrapped himself around her was enough to comfort her and lull her to sleep.

Sometime later, Aubrey woke to Henry's voice. He was talking with someone in whispered anger. She felt the bed shift as he stood and his footsteps thudded against the floor in what she assumed was pacing. She didn't want to turn and let him know she was awake. She didn't want to be awake. She just wanted to go back to sleep for just a little longer. She didn't want to think about anything for just a little longer.

Aubrey closed her eyes, hoping to force her body into submission but it was no use. She turned over and looked up at Henry, his muscular frame pacing her room with one hand holding his cell to his ear and the other gesturing wildly. It would have looked completely normal had he still been wearing his suit. But doing so in his Superman boxers made her giggle.

Henry's eyes cut to hers and he gave her a small smile. Someone was talking on the other end, and when Henry's smile disappeared, she knew that whatever he was hearing wasn't what he wanted.

"I don't care that we did to land the company. What I care about is HOW we got them. We are not a corrupt business. We do not lie and cheat to gain clients. If they can't trust us, then we might as well close our doors now while we're ahead."

His pacing stopped, but the irritation etched on his face grew into rage. His quiet angered words were nothing compared to the bark that came out next. "Tell that bitch that she will never work for Maximus. I don't care if you already hired her, fire her, and pack your own desk while you're at it!"

Henry stabbed at the screen of his phone with his finger before throwing it across the room into the chair that held his clothing. He sat back on the bed and ran both hands through his hair, gripping and pulling when he had a handful.

"So I take it Maximus Gaming had an interesting day at the office, too?"

"It was Jenna. She made a deal with my acquisition's guy for a job if she could get Keith to switch companies. She called him last night, and he set up the teleconference for this morning. I am so sorry, Aubrey. I don't know how many times I have to say it, but I will. Over and over. I wonder how many other deals we made that weren't on the up and up. I thought he was a better person than that."

"It isn't your fault. It's Jenna's. I can't believe I worked with her for so long and didn't know how vile she could be. She thought I was after her job. I didn't want her job even though I could do it ten times better than she could. I like doing the research and coming up with fun ideas for marketing. I thought I was pretty good at it, too. Too bad both companies I was able to pitch to didn't sign with us."

Henry let out a sigh. "Again, sorry about that."

"Don't. I knew working at Viola and you owning our biggest competition would cause problems. I just thought it would be a relationship issue, ya know, not being able to talk about the biggest part of our day could really kill the communication and all. I supposed I should go grab the damn paper and start looking through the want ads."

"Or we could stay right here for a while and pretend that the only problem we have is the limited amount of time before your brother and Mackenna get home." Henry hovered over her on the bed and leaned down slowly, hovering with his lips just above hers.

"I think that's doable," she said then pressed her lips against his.

Henry's hands worked her body into a frenzy, bringing her to the brink only to tease her by pulling back. He tickled and licked her ribs, causing her to crumble in a fit of erotic giggles before he finally pinned her hands above her head and looked at her with such passion and want in his eyes that even he could no longer fight it.

Aubrey opened her legs, letting Henry's body fall between them. With a swift movement of his hips, he sank himself deep within her, eliciting a moan from deep in her chest. With her arms positioned above her, all she could do was stare at him, feel him. He leaned in again, kissing her and at the same time released her hands. Aubrey quickly wrapped them around his body, caressing his back and touching him wherever she could reach as he rhythmically brought their hips together. The passion built inside of her with every wave of his hips like an ocean lapping at the sand in a storm, getting faster and stronger as every second passed until it finally crashed.

Aubrey's scream tore through the apartment and both of their breaths were labored as their bodies calmed from the storm. He leaned in again, kissing her softly, and something in the way he looked at her made Aubrey's heart soar.

"I suppose we should get up. Things to do and all," he said while still hovering over her.

"I suppose we should," Aubrey looked at the clock and saw they still had hours until Ben and Mackenna came home, "or we could go back to sleep for an hour."

"You mean lay here with you wrapped up in my arms for another hour and pretend that the world outside that door doesn't exist? Let me think about that," he said with a grin then rolled off her. Henry's arms wrapped around her waist and pulled her to him. The paper would still be there in an hour, Ben and Mackenna still would be at school, and Henry was there, in her bed, holding her close. She was going to take every little bit of happy she could get. She hated the feeling gnawing in her gut that said to enjoy it now, because just like everything else, it wouldn't last.

When Aubrey woke, her arms instinctively reached over to the space beside her. When she felt the cool cotton beneath her fingers instead of Henry's warm skin, her heart raced. Had he left already? She knew it was too good to be true, but she at least expected him to wait to say goodbye.

A tear slipped from her eye as she thought about everything that had happened between them that day. What had she done? She lost her job and created a PR nightmare. Maybe she was more trouble than he thought she was worth. Aubrey looked over to her dresser to see the box that held Henry's comic book. She still hadn't been able to give it to him. Now she never would. What a waste of money. Money that she realized should have been saved for a rainy day because it sure as hell was storming.

The ache inside of her was all consuming. A little monster was digging at her chest with razor sharp claws from the inside out. It was shouting at her, over powering her mind with words like failure, stupid, idiot. She threw away her career for a man. A man that threw her away when things got tough.

The single tear that had rolled down her cheek was soon accompanied by another and another until Aubrey sat, naked and alone in her bed, sobbing.

Her bedroom door was thrown open, and much to her surprise, Henry ran in, jumping onto the bed, only to envelop her in his arms. The two rocked back and forth, her still sobbing even knowing that Henry was still there, and him shushing her and caressing anywhere he could reach.

Once she had calmed down, Henry pulled back and looked her in the eyes with such gentle worry. "What happened, baby?"

"I thought you—"

Only she couldn't finish the sentence. She looked away, ashamed of her reaction. She had thought the worst in him instead of taking the time to actually look for him. She was an idiot.

"You thought I what? Left?"

She nodded in response, and Henry sighed.

"Aubrey, look at me." When she didn't comply, Henry moved his position to put himself in front of her. "I am not going anywhere. I'm right here."

She nodded again, still unsure of her voice, and hugged him. She had been wrong, but that heart wrenching, stomach clenching feeling wasn't something she ever wanted to feel again. She couldn't let him get any closer than he already was.

"Come on, I ordered lunch. There's pizza and wings in the kitchen. There's supposed to be a Batman marathon on the cartoon channel today. I can introduce you to one of my past times while we eat."

Aubrey looked up to see the hopefulness etched on his face.

"I guess we can do that. Or you can watch your men in tights, and I will scan the want ads."

"I figured you might say that. The table also has four different newspapers covering a twenty mile radius."

"Thank you."

Aubrey gathered her clothing and got dressed again. She wanted to stay in the city. She wanted to find another job that day, but knowing her luck, and the parade of paparazzi that had been following her, job hunting might not go so well.

She grabbed the comic book off the top of her dresser and turned to Henry. "Here, I got this for you," she said and handed it over, and then walked out of the bedroom. She still wanted him to have it, but she didn't want to make it a big emotional scene like the one she originally envisioned. They had had enough heart to hearts in last few days, and she didn't need another that would put Henry Maximus any deeper under her skin or in her heart.

Chapter Eighteen

Aubrey had started to plate their lunch on the paper plates she kept in the kitchen cabinet. They hadn't gotten any real dishes yet except for a pot and a frying pan. She was perfectly okay with disposable. It cut down on dishes and arguments in the house over whose turn it was to clean them.

"Thank you," Henry said from the doorway. She turned to him and saw that he wore a guarded smile. He could tell she was pulling away, she just knew it. She was actually a little glad he had noticed. That way he could protect himself from the inevitable, too. She never wanted to see him hurting. She never wanted to be the cause of his pain. It would crush her. Better if they both keep enough distance to protect their hearts, but stay close enough to be happy. There had to be a way.

"You're welcome. Here, have some lunch." She smiled at him and handed the plate over. She didn't want to end what they had. She hoped he understood that. Henry walked forward with a slight look of worry and took the plate from her. She leaned over and kissed his cheek as he went by.

"Do you want me to call Mr. Fredrickson? I can explain what happened. Maybe he will hire you back."

"No. It wouldn't do any good."

"Shouldn't they know about Jenna? Shouldn't they know that you didn't sell the company out? You don't want that on your resume. It isn't true."

"We both know it isn't. This is just how my life goes, Henry. I'm used to it. If you plan on sticking around, you should get used to it to. Nothing good lasts long when I'm involved. Nothing."

"Bullshit. Stop the pity party and get angry. You got screwed over by Jenna. You should want her to pay for it. And what we have is good. And hear me when I say, I. Am. Not. Going. Anywhere."

"Pity party? Great. Thanks. Call him if you want, but don't be surprised when he tells you to pound salt."

"One day you will realize that this isn't your life. Failure isn't what or who you are. You only fail if you stop trying and stop picking yourself back up. Are you at least going to call Bridgette?"

"What is there to say? We weren't as close as I thought. She would have come to say goodbye if we were. She didn't. I'm not going to call and beg her to be my friend. It hurt enough realizing she wasn't. Why put myself through that again?"

"Have you learned nothing? Don't push her away, too. Maybe she has a good reason. Give her a chance. Give yourself a chance, Aubrey."

"Fine." Aubrey agreed and walked back into the bedroom, shutting the door behind her. She sat on the edge of the bed with her phone in her hands. She would call because she told Henry she would, and she wanted to be the person he believed her to be. But first, she had to get her head and heart in a place where no matter what Bridgette had to say wouldn't hurt her. The longer she sat there, the more she realized she wasn't going to be able to do that. With a deep breath, she scrolled through her contacts and pressed call.

The phone rang once, twice, and a third time. Maybe Bridgette wouldn't answer. That would give her an answer and keep the embarrassment to a minimum. But then, on the fifth ring, she picked up.

"Hey," Bridgette said in a soft voice.

"Hey," Aubrey replied.

"Look"—

"Wait, just listen, okay? I need to know why you bailed on me. I need to know if we were actually friends or just co-workers who hung out once in a while. Where were you?" Aubrey asked, barely holding the tears back. Damn it, she hadn't wanted to get emotional.

"I couldn't. When the floor went crazy with the news, I tried to get down to the conference room but when Mike came up he gave me a ton of phone calls and told me if I stepped foot in the conference room I was as good as fired, too. I'm so sorry, but I couldn't risk that. I wanted to call you, but he was watching me the whole day, and then I saw all the news clips and stuff, and I thought that maybe you would want to be left alone. Aubrey, please know I don't believe what they are saying. You believe me, right?"

Relief flooded through her. Bridgette hadn't given up on her. "I do. What the hell am I going to do now?"

"I don't know, but you will figure it out. You worked your way up faster than anyone I have ever seen. You will do it again. And now you have a hot ass man by your side to be a shoulder when you need to scream and cry about starting over. And you can call me whenever, and we can still go dancing together. Just because we don't work together doesn't mean we're done. You're stuck with me now," she said with a laugh.

Aubrey thanked her and told her once her life settled down they would get together and hung up. She walked out of the room with a smile. She knew she should thank Henry for making her call, but the smile he gave her when they locked eyes told her no thanks was needed. He understood.

"Come on, I have an entire series to introduce you to." He motioned with his head to follow him into the living room.

Aubrey grabbed her plate off the table and one of the papers. She followed him over to the newly finished futon couch that Ben and Mackenna had been fighting over. It was actually quite comfortable. "Guess Mackenna can do something right," she said with an eye roll.

"Oh, is this the couch they were fighting over?" he asked, shocking Aubrey that he actually remembered the conversation.

"Yeah, it is. You remember that?"

"Of course, it was important to you."

The knot in her stomach twisted and tightened with his words. They made her heart soar and that was not good. Space, they needed space. Boundaries. He shouldn't be allowed to say those things to her. If she didn't respond, maybe he would understand.

"So, Batman?"

"Aubrey?"

"Hmm?" she took a bite of pizza, hoping a full mouth would stop the conversation she knew was coming.

"Stop. I told you, I'm not going anywhere. We had come so far. You let me in. Don't push me out now."

"I don't want you to go, I just don't want to hurt when I screw everything up and make you want to leave. You say you won't now, but I won't be enough. Or I'll say something stupid and piss you off, or your company will become an international conglomerate, and you have to move to some place like Zimbabwe or Germany or Japan. What then? Wouldn't it be better to enjoy each other while we can but keep ourselves from falling into a million pieces when it ends?"

"Why does it have to end? Why would you think that you could ever do anything to make me stop—"

Henry wasn't able to finish his sentence because the door to the apartment flew open, and Ben and Mackenna raced inside. Aubrey was glad, too. She wasn't ready to hear what he was about to say.

"We'll finish this later. Okay?" Henry said, holding her hand in his. Again, she answered with a nod.

She didn't want to finish it. If she heard him say what she thought he was going to, she wouldn't be able to pretend she didn't feel that way, too. She wouldn't be able to keep him at arms length. And she would get hurt in a way she wasn't sure she would come back from.

"Why are you home?" Ben asked through deep breaths.

"That's kinda what I need to talk to you to about. Come on, grab some pizza, and sit down."

"So, is this Mr. Billionaire?" Mackenna asked with a tilt to her head and a fluttering of her eyelashes. "Kinda hot in that geeky Clark Kent kind of way."

"Um," Henry looked to Aubrey for help. She was irritated at Mackenna for what she said, but wanted to laugh at Henry's reaction to it.

"That's enough, Mackenna." Aubrey shook her head and waited for the two to come and sit down. Mackenna managed to sit as close to Henry as possible without actually sitting on him. Ben watched with a careful eye that Aubrey could see was actually twitching every time Mackenna accidentally brushed Henry's arm. "So, you know the insanity that started this morning. I hate to say it only got worse. Viola let me go."

Aubrey didn't want to mention Henry's company in any of it. He was already shouldering the blame because it was one of his employees that had been less than ethical, and she didn't want Ben to blame him, too. After all, Ben worked for Maximus. And he was the only one employed.

"Are you kidding me? What the hell did you do this time? What are we going to do?" Mackenna screeched.

"That's enough, Mackenna!" Ben yelled. Aubrey was shocked but glad that Ben was standing up to her. He had grown up a lot since they found out about the baby, and unfortunately, Mackenna hadn't.

"Shut up, Ben. You think your minimum wage fifteen hours a week is going to keep us in this apartment? The bills are Aubrey's responsibility, and she just fucked up."

"If you can't act like an adult, you can leave the conversation and start packing your shit now. I am tired of the way you treat my brother and me. My parents were right to tell you no to moving in. I am sorry that your parents kicked you out, but I can't handle you if you are going to act like a fucking child. Grow up or get out. Those are your choices."

Aubrey was waiting for Ben to say something, to disagree or argue her case, but he didn't. He didn't say a word and that shocked her. It also shocked Mackenna who sat there and stared at him, waiting for him to say something. "Fine." She gritted out through her teeth. Her arms crossed over her chest and threw herself against the back of the couch.

"What happened?" Ben asked in a much calmer tone.

"I didn't get the contract. And they don't like me dating Henry."

"Okay, so what do we do now? Do we have enough for rent next month?"

"Rent yes, any other bill? Not really. I need to get a job and fast."

"You know I can help as long as you need me to," Henry offered. Mackenna's face lit up, and she sat forward with a smile.

"See, problem solved!" she squealed.

"No, not solved. Henry, I appreciate the offer, but you know I can't take your money. I'm sure we will figure it out." She couldn't take his money. It wasn't right. She had to prove to herself that she could figure it out. She refused to fail again, and accepting his money felt like failure.

"Will you at least let me help you find a job? I have a lot of connections."

"That we can do."

"Mackenna, you need to get a job. No ifs, and, or buts about it. We all need to work together on this."

"But—"

"No, Mackenna! That was the deal from the beginning. Just get a damn job." Ben stormed out of the room. Aubrey looked to Henry and bit her lip. She needed to go talk to Ben, but didn't want to leave him with Mackenna.

"Go," he said, softly. Aubrey leaned over and kissed his cheek and followed Ben into their bedroom.

~*~

Aubrey knocked on the bedroom door, softly. She could hear Ben in there throwing things around. He wrenched the door open, irritation clear on his face.

"Hey, can we talk?" she asked, waiting for him to dismiss her. She knew her brother. She knew when he was in a mood he usually wanted to be left alone, but this was different.

"Yeah, come on in." He walked away from her and continued to pick things up. Aubrey closed the door behind her and saw what he was doing. He was putting Mackenna's things into boxes.

"What are you doing?"

"Packing her shit up. She isn't going to grow up or get a job. What kind of mom is she going to be? How am I going to be able to afford this baby alone? When we started talking about keeping her, we said we would do it together. That we would both work to save as much as possible while she was pregnant, and then as soon as she could, she would go back to work. She was going to apply at day cares and stuff, so she could bring the baby."

Ben stopped packing and sat on the bed. He was just as dejected as the day he sat on her bed and told her about the baby to begin with. Aubrey sat beside him and wrapped him in her arms just like that day.

"If she had told me back then that she was going to abort, or even give the baby up for adoption, I would have gone along with her. What the hell did I know about babies or working or any of that? But now? I love that little baby even though she's still so damn tiny. How can I love her already?"

"Because she's yours. And you have grown up so much, Ben. It's not going to be easy, I don't think it ever will be, but you can do this. You know I will help in every way I can."

"You think it's a girl, too?" he asked in a whisper.

"Yeah, I do."

"Mackenna wants a boy."

"We'll just have to wait for the sonogram to find out for sure, won't we?"

"What do I do if she doesn't get a job? Do I let her leave alone, or do I move with her?"

"That's up to you, Ben. But I can't let her act like that."

"I know."

"Would I be horrible if I stayed with you? Do you even want me to now that you have lover boy out there?"

"You wouldn't be horrible. You would be horrible if you turned your back on the baby. But you aren't, and you can stay with me as long as you want. I have my own room so Henry and I don't really need to be factored into your equation."

"Well, if I need to invest in some super strength ear plugs you do."

Aubrey's jaw dropped and Ben let out a boisterous laugh. They had heard, and apparently, the brother-sister heart to heart was over in favor of the teasing she had been waiting to start since morning. She threw a pillow at him and left the room.

Chapter Nineteen

Two weeks. Two weeks had gone by and every single lead that Aubrey had for a job was squashed. The media circus had died down the minute the "it" couple of Hollywood had broken up. Aubrey had never been so thankful for an actor sloppily cheating on his wife in all her life. But that didn't mean that all the corporations hadn't seen the disaster that was her life just weeks prior. Even Henry's contacts gave her a polite 'No thank you'.

"More coffee?" Henry asked from the kitchen, holding up a pot. He stood there in his suit looking all sorts of delicious. He had spent more than half the nights with her, and she was still waiting for the shoe to drop. Henry had carefully kept all conversations away from anything emotionally serious, and for that, Aubrey was grateful.

"Yes please. I have to go get applications for retail places today. I've put it off long enough. The corporate world isn't going to care that I worked my ass off for a company that fired me. I don't have a degree so on the job training is meaningless. Good thing I know how to fold clothes, right?" she asked in a mock cheerfulness.

"Are you sure—"

"Stop right there. I can fold clothing or flip burgers, or ring a cash register just fine. I can work my butt off and learn a new industry and prove to whatever company that hires me that I am worth training to move up. Henry, I can't take your money. Okay?"

"I know you're going through some crap right now, but I have to know that we are okay. Please don't push me away now." Henry's eyes were focused on her, confusion and hurt written across his face.

"We're okay. Promise." Aubrey couldn't tell him she wasn't pushing him away. She couldn't lie. But she wasn't exactly pushing. It was more like keeping them in the same place. No closer than they already were. She knew she felt things that hadn't been said aloud, and she wanted to keep it that way. The minute they said anything like those stupid words out loud, everything would go to shit.

"Okay. I have to go," he said and moved to kiss her goodbye. His lips still sent tingles straight to her nether regions even after so many of them and that made her smile. "I'll see you later."

"Bye," she said and watched him walk out the door. She sighed and made a list of places to go after she finished her coffee.

~*~

Aubrey stood at a counter filling out a paper application while waiting for the manager to come to the front. The clothing store she stood in was trendy and hip and meant for the teenage crowd. Once upon a time, this would have been her dream job. But in that moment, she felt so dejected.

When the manager approached, a girl that couldn't have even been old enough to buy a drink without a fake ID, she was wearing tight fitting jeans and a t-shirt that said 'Parental Advisory' on it. She looked at the girl's obvious confusion and looked down at herself. Apparently her skirt suit wasn't quite fitting for this type of job hunt.

"Can I help you?" she asked.

"I just wanted to introduce myself and give you my application and resume personally." Aubrey held the papers out to the girl who took them with a smile.

"Thanks, I'll add them to the stack. I'll give you a call if something opens up. Have a great day!"

The manager turned and headed into the office with her papers. Aubrey sighed dejectedly and started for the front of the store. The clothing in there was fashionable but it was the same stuff that had been out the year before. Aubrey looked around a bit before heading out and to her next location.

Aubrey climbed into her car and grabbed her phone. She purposefully left it behind knowing that a ringing phone would be unprofessional if she happened to get an on the spot interview. Waiting for her was a text from Henry.

I know you want to stay in the city but there is a small house for rent down the street from me. Maybe you should check it out.

She didn't want to leave the city but rent was due in two weeks. If they paid it, they wouldn't have light or even much for groceries. She wasn't sure how it would work job wise either, but with no other options, she knew she needed to look. While she was in town, she would stop and talk to her parents about moving back into the attic. Again. Maybe they would let her borrow the cash it would cost for a moving truck. She would never take money from Henry, but her parents were another story.

I'll look. Need to prep the parents for the attic invasion anyway.

Want me to meet you there?

Up to you.

Part of her wanted him there but another wanted to do it on her own. But every time she went to answer one way or the other, she thought of a reason not to. So instead, she would let him pick. She was pretty sure she knew his answer before he even sent it.

See you in an hour.

Aubrey drove the familiar rode from the city into the country and into the little town she never managed to really get away from. Was she meant for small town life? Was this the universes way of telling her to stop fighting it? It wasn't that bad, she had just always envisioned the city as this glamorous place to live and work. But that was the thing. Living in the city without a job wasn't glamorous. It was scary and damn near impossible.

She drove through town and saw the little clothing shop that Henry had told her about on her first visit to his house, the one that she was supposed to get new clothes from but never did. If they were new, maybe they needed a cashier. It would beat the gas costs of driving to and from the city every day. She made it work before, but with a lower paying job and actual bills, she wasn't really sure the city was the best place to work if she took the place Henry had found for her.

The store front was similar to all the other little shops on the street, made of brick with big glass windows and a hanging sign in front of the door. Aubrey could picture it with mannequins in the windows and colorful signs. It could really be eye catching with the right changes.

She climbed out of the car and walked in, the bell ringing as the door opened and closed behind her. The clothes were cute, and fresh, and could work for teenagers and twenty-somethings, alike. The owner had it split up into day wear and business wear, and Aubrey found herself wishing she had extra cash to blow. Why hadn't she heard about this place before?

"Welcome! If you need any help just let me know."

"Hi!" Aubrey said with excitement. "This is some really great stuff you have here."

"Thanks, I design it all myself."

"You're Leena, right? I think we went to school together."

"Yup, that's me. And you're Aubrey."

"I am, and I am moving back to the area." Aubrey gave Leena the resume she had brought in with her. "I would like to apply for a position if you are hiring."

"I wish I could help you. But I barely have enough to keep the doors open. I work the store on my own."

Aubrey sighed. Of course she couldn't. Small town girl in a small town shop. Too bad her designs were so good. If Aubrey could get a hold of her marketing, she could seriously take her places. Then she perked up. She could help her with marketing!

"Leena, have you thought about marketing at all?"

"I don't have the funds to really do too much. I mean, I posted in the local paper and sent a notice to the paper in the city, but it didn't do much."

"What if I came up with a marketing plan for you that didn't break the bank but brought in a ton of new customers? Would you consider hiring me then? I could help run the store so you could have days off, and I could be in charge of marketing and taking your name and clothing to the big time."

"Like a trial? You would do the marketing plan for free, and if it worked, then I hire you?"

"Right. Give me a week. I need a job and you need help. You know that means I will work my butt off for you."

Aubrey waited in silence while Leena thought over her offer. She was already envisioning an online campaign and setting up a website for sales and a fashion show at the high school. So many ideas were swimming through her head! She was getting excited.

"Okay. One week."

"Thank you. You won't regret it!"

Aubrey left the store and practically raced over to Henry's street. He was standing outside a tiny little blue house with a large front yard and a fenced in back yard. It had white shutters and a white door, and it looked like a little fairy tale.

Aubrey had seen the house before. It had been there for as long as she could remember. But it always had someone living in it. She had always loved the way it looked and was surprised to see it was the house up for rent.

"This one? I have always loved this one!"

"Yes, this one. The family that was here before moved away, not sure why. But whatever the reason, it's good, right? You want to look inside? The property manager is waiting inside for you. Ben is already in there looking around."

"You brought Ben? But I thought he was on shift all day?"

"Eh, it's a Saturday, and I already told him if he wanted to make up the hours, he could work tomorrow in the copy room since the coffee cart is closed. Plus, not many people are in the office, and he should see it too. Maybe convince Mackenna to help out."

"Let's not talk about Mackenna. Come on, let's go in."

The house was small but perfect. There were actually three bedrooms. The master had a jetted tub that Mackenna was drooling over and the third bedroom was small but perfect for a baby's room. The backyard had fully grown fruit trees and plenty of space. The price tag per month was what really sealed the deal. It was half the cost of her apartment.

She just needed to kill the marketing plan and get that job.

Chapter Twenty

Aubrey was never happier for a month to month lease in her life. When they first got the apartment it was the one drawback because that meant they could up the rent at any time. But right then, it was their saving grace. Without it, she could have had to pay serious fines for leaving after only two months.

Two months. Her 'success' had lasted all of two months. But it didn't matter. She had the perfect marketing plan made out for Leena. She had already found models who work in trade, she found a web developer at the University in the city to create a web page as long as they got to use it for their senior project, and an entire years worth of projected numbers ready and waiting. At least this time she wasn't competing against anyone but herself for the job.

The last box was loaded into the tiny moving truck they rented, and Aubrey climbed into her car. Henry was taking Ben to the new house to start unloading, and she was going to Leena. With one last look in her rear view mirror at the apartment building, she took off.

The music was blasting through the radio, and Aubrey sang along at the top of her lungs, letting herself feel the music and let go of the stress that had been holding her so tight she almost couldn't breathe. She just knew that this was going to be her turning point. She was never all that interested in video games, but she loved the marketing side. She was good at coming up with ways to appeal to the masses in new and unique ways, even when she didn't get the product. Clothing she got. Especially, Leena's line. The clothing that Leena was able to come up with made her job easy.

Aubrey parked the car in front of the little shop and went in with a stack of files and folders. Each folder was a different strategy, but they all worked together. The bell rang as the door opened, and Leena came out of the back room with a big smile on her face.

"You came!"

"Of course I did. I told you I was going to create a marketing plan for you, and I did. And most of it won't cost you a dime."

"Most of it?" Leena asked skeptically, leading Aubrey over to a counter near the back wall. She was expecting the comment. Leena had already mentioned being cash strapped, so Aubrey came up with the least expensive options but even those had some costs involved.

"Yes, most of it. So here's my plan. First, we get you a website and do a social media blitz. The costs here are minimal. A yearly fee for your domain, and a small monthly fee for your hosting. Or, you could pay for a year or two of hosting up front to get a discount."

"But who is going to design it? I have no skills in that stuff. My design skills are purely fabric based."

"That's the best part. I contacted the University in the city. There is a senior who needs a project for her to be able to graduate. Her major is graphic design for web development. As long as she can put your page in her portfolio, leave a link to her business page on your page, and use the statistics that start coming in for your page in her final presentation in ten months, she will design it free of charge."

"That's great, Aubrey! What else?" Aubrey could see a fire in her eyes that she hadn't seen before. She was getting excited and that made Aubrey smile. She went on to explain how she wanted to do a fashion show at the high schools around the area, charging for tickets, but donating the money right back to the school. She showed Leena the projected sales to come from the website and the added traffic to the store from the local schools and the tax benefits of the donations. If everything went according to plan, Leena's shop should actually make money by the years end.

"I guess I need you to pick out an outfit or two. If you're going to be working here, you need to be wearing my line. I can start you and pay you as a cashier to begin with. Once the sales come in, we can change your pay."

Aubrey smiled at Leena so big her cheeks hurt. "Thank you."

"If this works, I need to thank you."

Aubrey looked around for a bit before choosing a few items and insisting on paying for them. Leena gave her a discount and told Aubrey not to fight it. Employees got discounts at plenty of places, and she wouldn't take no for an answer. The women said goodbye and made plans for Aubrey to begin working the following Monday.

She couldn't stop smiling the whole way home.

~*~

Pulling up to the blue house felt like a dream. Ben and Henry were working together to unload the moving truck. Her parents were standing in the yard, looking around the house and smiling. And for a brief second, Aubrey pictured this being her life forever. And that thought didn't scare her.

Aubrey climbed out of the car and went to her parents. She had called them after deciding to take the house. It had been too long since they spoke, and she knew that ignoring the problem wasn't going to make it go away. She apologized for being a brat and for not trusting their judgment on Mackenna. She explained what had been happening and asked for their advice. They told her to stick to her guns, and if Mackenna didn't do what she promised, not to let her move into the blue house with them.

And she did. Mackenna went back to her parents and begged them to let her come home. Apparently, they had been trying to contact her for a while to ask her to return home but she had been ignoring them, hurt over their reaction to the baby.

"Hey, what do you think?" she asked her father. He looked over to Henry then back to her.

"I think you made a good choice." His sly smile told her he wasn't talking about the house. As much as the thought scared her before, she was beginning to see that she didn't really have much choice as to how close Henry got. She tried to push him away and he wouldn't let her. She tried to stay away and her heart hurt so much that she had to run right back to him.

"I think so, too." She hugged her father and then her mother. Aubrey walked through the gate into the back yard. Maybe one day her little niece would have a cousin to play with back there. Aubrey went to the tree and saw the little buds that would turn to apples in a few short months. She smiled thinking of picking apples with little kids.

Arms wrapped around her waist and warm breath tickled her ear. She sighed and leaned back into Henry's body, trusting him to support her.

"How'd it go?" he asked then kissed the spot right behind her ear. A shiver went through her body and she turned in his arms to look him in the eyes.

"I got it. She loved my ideas."

"I knew she would."

"You did, didn't you?" Henry smiled and nodded at her. Looking into his eyes and being in that yard in his arms felt so right, for the first time, she felt like she had more than just the job right. She had her life right. She wasn't failing at anything except for failing to follow her heart. She had a job doing what she loved. She had a place to call home that wasn't her parent's house. She was on good terms with her whole family at the same time. And she was wrapped up in the arms of the most perfect man she had ever met—Superhero t-shirts, and all.

She was done pushing. She was ready to pull him close and hold on for as long as he let her.

"I love you, Henry."

His eyes went wide but only for a second. His smile radiated, and his arms tightened around her, pressing their bodies against each other completely. Henry leaned in and pressed his lips to hers.

When he pulled back, he looked at her with utter joy and said, "I love you, too."

About the Author

Growing up, Adrianne couldn't get her hands on enough books to satisfy her need for the make believe. If she finished a novel and didn't have a new one ready and waiting for her, she began to create her own tales of magic and wonder. Now, as an adult, books still make up majority of her free time, and now her tales get written down to be shared with the world.

During the day, Adrianne uses her camera to capture life's stories for clients of all ages and at night, after her two children are tucked in bed; she devotes herself to her written work. Adrianne is living the life she always wanted, surrounded by art and beauty, the written word and a loving family.

As a young adult and new adult author, Adrianne James has plans to bring stories of growing characters, a little romance, and perhaps a little magic and mythology down the line for her readers to enjoy.